CUT NUMBERS

BOOKS BY NICK TOSCHES

Country
Hellfire
Unsung Heroes of Rock 'n' Roll
Power on Earth

CUT NUMBERS.

NICK TOSCHES

HARMONY BOOKS
NEW YORK

FOR HER
"caelestis, fellat et inspirat"

Copyright © 1988 by Nick Tosches, Inc.

All rights reserved. No part of this book may be reproduced or transmitted in any form or by any means, electronic or mechanical, including photocopying, recording, or by any information storage and retrieval system, without permission in writing from the publisher.
Published by Harmony Books, a division of Crown Publishers, Inc., 225 Park Avenue South, New York, New York 10003 and represented in Canada by the Canadian MANDA Group
HARMONY and colophon are trademarks of Crown Publishers, Inc.
Manufactured in the United States of America

Library of Congress Cataloging-in-Publication Data

Tosches, Nick.
Cut numbers.
I. Title.
PS3570.O74C88   1988   813'.54   88-899
ISBN 0-517-56870-5
10 9 8 7 6 5 4 3 2 1
First Edition

*TRUST AND MISTRUST
ALIKE RUIN MEN.*
                    HESIOD

Clouds like gusted shadows of the dead moved past the Lenten moon, drifting west toward Jersey. Louie saw them.

The suitcase was heavy and unwieldy. As he came to Varick Street, he put it down. He rubbed the fingers and palm of his right hand with his left. He lighted a cigarette, lifted the case, and continued on his way. He walked slowly, not to lull the clanking of his load, but because night's end was for him the best part of the day. All was quiet except for the waking gray birds and the faint drone of scattered tunnel traffic. He felt strong and serene, unconquerable, if only for a breath or two, in the face of the coming day's inevitable attrition. Black became deepest blue, and the one star he saw vanished before him. He crossed Sixth Avenue. The church campanile came into sight. Deepest blue became day, and Louie entered the Street of Silence, where he was no longer alone.

A fading middle-aged woman stood near the curb, looking away as her leashed black animal released a long amber jet onto the tire of a parked Cutlass Ciera. Some yards away, from a building across the street, another woman emerged. She was younger, and her looks bespoke a greater devotion to the illusion of well-being. Her stretch pants and tent blouse were neatly ironed, and her hair was done in a silvered flip, similar to that worn by the model in the Alberto VO-5 placard in the window of Ralph's Mona Lisa Beauty Salon. She, too, had a dog, a small white poodle. The two women greeted each other like weary patrol partners on a doomed, senseless mission.

A nearby door creaked. The man called Il Capraio appeared. The women lowered their heads and silently walked away. Il Capraio looked after them. He saw Louie approaching, but he did not acknowledge him. Slowly, almost imperceptibly, he shook his head in what may have been an expression of annoyance, or perhaps disgust. He inhaled deeply, as if he had been burdened no less in the last moments than God had been throughout all time. Then he turned and disappeared behind the creaking door.

Louie passed by that door, not turning to look at it or at the adjoining black-curtained storefront, which peeling gold-leaf lettering alleged to be the Ziginette Society of Sciacca. A few yards farther, he opened the door of another curtained front and walked in.

It was dark. Al Martino's version of "Daddy's Little Girl" played distortedly on the jukebox. Four barstools were occupied by human figures in similar states of dissolution. Two of them were completely still, their heads down. Another leaned back, his arms folded across his stomach, staring at the glass of clear liquor before him. The fourth, the fancier of "Daddy's Little Girl," moved his head and emitted a sickly quavering sound in dire harmony with the jukebox.

Louie said nothing as he walked past their backs. He knew them all, and he was gratified that he was not among them this morning. Savoring his strength amid their weakness, he strode straight to the end of the bar. There, poised above a plastic coffee cup, veiled in a haze of cigarette smoke, was a face as cold and hard and untelling as a sarcophagal effigy worn down by time to barest relief. The nose on this face had been broken so often, so long ago, that it could hardly be discerned. The thin mouth beneath it was turned implacably downward, and the nacreous eyes above it were wholly occluded by thick bifocal lenses. Sparse strands of white hair, lifeless as painted lines, traversed the cast of the old man's skull. With his head slightly raised, staring toward the door in stony vigilance, he seemed always to be awaiting the arrival, or the return, of some terrible, inevitable thing.

"Good morning, Giacomo," Louie said. He put down the suitcase and looked into the old man's bifocals. Only then did the old man move his head.

"Is that good Louie or bad Louie?" he asked. He peered through his spectacles into Louie's eyes and saw that they were clear and calm. "It's good Louie," he said, smiling.

Louie lifted the suitcase and carried it a few steps to the small Formica-topped table that stood in the darkness between the jukebox and the toilet. The old man followed him, shuffling resolutely on the worn linoleum floor. Grimacing, he raised his left arm, which suffered less from arthritis than his right. He grasped the string that hung overhead, and a bare bulb flooded the area with harsh light. Two of the figures at the bar stirred, then were silent again. One of them lifted his glass and drank.

Louie opened the suitcase. Giacomo methodically removed its contents: four bottles of Dewar's, four bottles of Johnnie Walker Red, four bottles of Smirnoff, one bottle of Martell V.S.O.P., one bottle of Bacardi Dark, one bottle of Southern Comfort. He held each bottle to the light and examined its seal. He took the last bottle from the suitcase. It was opaque beige in color, and it had a fluted neck. He squinted at it, then sneered dismally at Louie. "Praline Liqueur? What the fuck am I supposed to do with this?"

"Are you kiddin'? The broads love it. It's like Kahlúa, Irish Cream, that sort of shit."

Giacomo looked away. "A hundred and fifty," he said.

Louie nodded, and the old man reached deeply into his pants pocket. He brought out a handful of folded money and held it close to his face, extracting three fifties. He gave the bills to Louie, then began moving the bottles, two at a time, to the shelves that were situated out of sight beneath the back of the bar. As he lowered the last bottle, the Praline Liqueur, he shook his head and coughed.

"You want coffee?"

Louie nodded, and the old man shuffled to the three-pot Silex gas range against the wall. He poured two cups and put a teaspoon of sugar and some milk in one of them. He carried them carefully to the end of the bar, placing the one with the sugar and milk in it in front of Louie, then he came around the bar, settled with some exertion onto his chair, lighted a cigarette, and resumed his posture of grim vigilance. The two of them sat in silence, drinking coffee and smoking. After a while, the old man turned and peered at the clock over his shoulder. It was a quarter to seven.

"The happiness boys," he said, gesturing with his chin toward the four figures at the bar. He took a handkerchief from his back pocket and removed his spectacles. Louie saw that there were drops of teary blood at the corners of the old man's colorless eyes. The old man wiped at them with his handkerchief, then eased his spectacles back on. "Shit-head there looks like he's ready for Perazzo," he said, indicating the slumped form nearest the door. "He can barely lift the fuckin' glass." The old man ground out his cigarette and sipped his coffee. "He wasn't drinkin' for the longest time. He came in here the morning of the Super-bowl: 'Make it a short one, I got things to do.' Next morning, he's back, blown out of his socks. He's been burnin' with a low blue flame ever since. And this is, what, the first week of spring?"

"He's got money, then, huh?"

The old man increased his frown and shook his head. "A

4

few bucks at first, but he's been runnin' a tab for weeks now. They're all on the muldoon, the four of 'em. If it wasn't for the young crowd, there'd be nothin' here lately."

"I figured the other asshole there'd be lyin' on the beach down there on that island he goes to."

"Ain't he a piece of work, though? He sticks up that fuckin' jukebox joint in Queens, then he sits around here playin' that 'Daddy's Little Girl' for a month. 'You're givin' it all back,' I told him. 'Nah,' he says, 'it's a different outfit.' How do you talk to somebody like that? 'Listen to the words,' he tells me. 'I used to sing it to my daughter.' You know his daughter? That pig that the sanitation guys used to hump?" The old man scratched his neck and put another cigarette in his mouth. "And get a load of Sleepin' Beauty over here. He's ready for a fuckin' room with a view on the East River."

"He owes me, that bastard," Louie said. "He's been dodgin' me for months."

"Points?"

"No. It was only a hundred, thirty cents on a dollar. He was supposed to pay off in five weeks at twenty-six a shot. He made two payments. Since then, *domani, domani.*"

The old man grinned. "Loan him another couple yards so he can pay his tab." Louie uttered a low guttural sound and grinned back at him.

The old man looked again at the clock, then he stood. "It is now post time," he announced. He strode firmly to the front of the room, drew back the window curtains, and raised the shade on the door. The bar filled with daylight. The old man leaned at the window, looking out. A young woman in a blue suit and white blouse walked briskly by, clutching her briefcase and averting her eyes from the window.

"Look at the ass on this one," Giacomo said, with something not unlike happiness in his voice. "Dressed for success. If only she knew." He nodded sternly, and there was nothing like happiness in his voice. "All these cute young girls with their big blue eyes, them and those boy-asses with the fancy haircuts, swaggerin' around like they're in one of them beer commercials on TV. They call these tenements co-ops. I swear, you could sell these kids shit on a stick if you came up with the right name for it. They'd buy the Brooklyn Bridge if you told 'em it was goin' condominium." The old man lighted another cigarette and blew smoke toward the window. "Someday, if they're lucky, they'll look up and see that co-op roof cavin' in and they'll realize they been carryin' thirty-year paper to live in some shit-hole that's been fallin' apart since Christ left Chicago, and they'll look in that mirror and see those gray hairs and all those new up-and-comers comin' up behind 'em; then they'll figure it out." He smoked and turned away. "Then again, who gives a fuck."

He slapped his hand down near where one man's head lay upon his folded arms. "Let's get this show on the road. Live people are comin' here soon." The head stirred. The old man moved down the bar, and one by one the other men were roused. They stretched, rubbed their faces, and nodded in miserable concession. They hailed Louie, seeing him now for the first time. The music lover reached inside his jacket and withdrew some crumpled dollars. He placed one of them on the bar, and he smoothed it with his hand.

"Quarters, Jocko. And another shot," he added, as if it were an afterthought.

"*Because you're daddy's little girl*," Giacomo sang from the side of his mouth. His hand came down on the dollar, and he grinned to Louie.

As the voice of Al Martino rose amid the loud violins and surface noise, the front door opened, and there entered a small, smiling man in a tan twill cap and coat.

"Good morning, all you beautiful people," he said, his

smile widening sardonically. He walked to the end of the bar, yelling "Sing it, you guinea bastard" as he passed the jukebox. He put a *Daily News* on the bar and rubbed his hands together. "In spring a young man's fancy turns to love. That's what they say."

Giacomo placed a spoon in a glass. He half-filled the glass with steaming coffee, then poured in Cutty Sark. He pushed the glass toward the small, smiling man.

"What was it?" the old man asked, after the little man had stirred and sipped.

"Nine-sixteen, Brooklyn. Three-eleven, New York."

"More cut numbers," Giacomo said. "What shit." He looked toward the window, receding into his dead vigilance.

The little man turned to Louie. "How's business, kid?"

"Business sucks," Louie said. "How's with you?"

The smile eased from the little man's face, and he breathed drearily. "I ain't had a hit in weeks," he said. He glanced at the jukebox, then at the music lover, then he drank. "This legal shit is killin' us. Everybody's playin' the fuckin' Lotto these days. Some days, the way things are goin', I think I'd be better off makin' the rounds with a shoeshine box." He finished his drink and pushed the empty glass forward, placing a ten-dollar bill beside it. With a fast flourish of his left hand, he indicated that he also wanted to buy coffee for Louie. Giacomo rose and filled the glass and pushed it back, then gave Louie a fresh cup of coffee. While he was up, he went to the switch beneath the counter. He flicked it twice and the volume of the jukebox, which now was playing "You Belong to Me" by Dean Martin, fell to a faint undertone. The music lover protested, but the old man just stared at him until he, too, quieted.

"Let's go to Martin's," the one nearest the door said.

"It ain't eight yet," the music lover said.

"Ah, fuck that joint," the third among them, the risen Sleeping Beauty, said. "Let's go to Brooklyn."

"Fuck Brooklyn," the fourth snarled. "You just wanna see that Irish cunt with the tits."

"I ain't goin' nowhere," the music lover said.

All of them except the music lover rose and gathered themselves to venture into society. As they did so, Louie also rose.

"Hey," he called.

The risen Sleeping Beauty turned. Louie beckoned him with his hand, then led him back to the Formica-topped table.

"What is this shit?" he whispered, looking into the other's downcast, reddened eyes.

"Things ain't been good."

"You're old enough to be my father and you're more stupid than I am. What is it with you?"

"Things, Louie, things." He drew slightly back as Louie moved closer.

"You make me look bad, you know that? I don't even really give a fuck about that. I don't. You know what I give a fuck about? I give a fuck about the fuckin' money. Seventy-eight dollars, I know, ain't nothin' to a bigshot like you. But to me seventy-eight dollars is seventy-eight dollars. And I want it. You hear me? I want it. That's it." Louie stared at him, seeing his breath grow deeper and his eyes become more and more like those of a child. "You shouldn't fuck your friends," Louie said at last, softly. The other nodded, and he muttered something. "Go on," Louie said, "try to straighten out. Do what you have to do, then come see me." He dismissed him with a sidewise toss of the head, then watched him join his two companions at the door.

"Always a pleasure." Giacomo waved to them as they left. He turned to Louie. "You're gettin' pretty good at that tough-guy shit, kid," he said, and grinned.

The small, smiling man took a long, final swallow, then smacked his lips. "Oh, well," he said, as he said every morning, "let me go. You want anything?"

The old man gave him two singles. "Four-oh-five, dollar straight, Brooklyn. Same thing, New York."

The smiling man held the dollars with one hand and scribbled with a short pencil onto a scrap of Yellow Freight System notepaper with the other.

Louie handed him a five: "One-eighty-seven for five, straight, Brooklyn."

The smiling man scribbled again, then put the money into the left pocket of his jacket, the pencil and paper into the right. He patted both pockets. "I'll see you people later," he said, then grinned and walked away. As he neared the door, it swung open. Three fat ladies huffed in, talking loudly and bringing with them the scent of Shalimar. "What was it?" one of them asked the little man in an urgent tone. He repeated the numbers: 916, Brooklyn; 311, New York. Winking toward the end of the bar, he hastened through the door.

"Three-eleven! My niece's birthday." The eldest of the women clicked her tongue. "I dreamt about her just the other night, too. Oh, well, what can you do."

Giacomo rose as the three women sat. He pressed three white plastic cups into three brown plastic holders and filled them.

"Hey, Jocko, gimme another fuckin' drink, huh?" the music lover called, pointing to his empty glass.

"Come on, watch your mouth. There's women here," the old man scolded. The fat ladies raised their eyebrows and moved their heads like bloated pigeons. The one who had dreamed of her niece primped her hair and clicked her tongue again. Giacomo placed the cups of coffee in front of them and collected the change that each of them had laid on the bar. He deposited the coins in the busted cash register, then tended to the music lover's drink.

"We gotta break it up after this one," he said. The music lover nodded, and the old man lowered his voice to a distinct whisper. "You oughta lay off this shit awhile, anyway. You're startin' to look like you could haunt houses for a livin'."

The old man poured himself another cup of coffee, then returned to the end of the bar, where he and Louie sat in silence and in smoke.

"I got sausage left over," one of the fat ladies announced, then nodded to herself. "I'll buy peppers."

"Green or red?" another said.

"You gotta be kiddin' me, red. Even the green are goin' through the ceiling." She sipped her coffee, then blew her nose.

The music lover muttered something. He finished his drink, raked his hand through his hair, and stood. He patted his belly and hoarsely bade good-bye.

"He was drunk, Jocko?" one of the women asked down the length of the bar. The old man shrugged.

"He was drunk," the oldest woman affirmed, pursing her lips and craning her neck knowingly. "You could tell by how he walked."

The fat ladies finished their coffee and inhaled tremulously.

"Good-bye, we'll see you tomorrow," one of them called. The others hoisted their waistbands and plucked through their blouses at the elastic cinctures of their brassieres. The door shut behind them, but the smell of Shalimar stayed.

"The old one, Mary, she still likes to fuck," Giacomo said. He began to laugh, but instead he coughed.

The room was silent then except for the sound of the old man's labored breath and the occasional ignitions of one or the other's cheap plastic lighter. Louie liked it like this:

the quiet and the coffee and the somber, soundless figures passing beyond the pane as in a dream. He watched the sea of motes that swirled in the sudden sunbeam at the end of the bar, and he thought of Donna Lou and the wild golden downy curls that fell free at the nape of her neck, escaping his grasp like mercurial light whenever he gathered her waves among the fingers of his fist to draw her head gently back or toward him. He did not see the sunbeam disappearing, swallowed by the passing clouds of March, and he did not see the nearer darkness at the door.

He heard the old man mutter something in a mean voice. Then he saw the door open. It was Il Capraio.

Neither Louie nor the old man let his eyes waver toward him; they just listened to the sound of his steps. And he did not look at them as he advanced, but strode directly to them with his head cast slightly downward, as if watching the line of a distant horizon. Then he stood beside them.

He was a medium-size man of about seventy years, with a small gut and thinning gray hair that he brushed straight back. He wore a light-blue polyester suit, which his father had died in some years ago, and a shirt that was the color of the Praline Liqueur bottle. As always, he wore no jewelry except a wedding ring, turned around so that its large diamond was in his fist.

"Coffee, Frank?" the old man said. Il Capraio waved his right hand in the negative and scowled.

"Nice out today," he said colorlessly.

Louie and Giacomo concurred in kind. Il Capraio lowered his chin, then raised it. He addressed Louie: "You gonna be seeing your uncle?"

"Tomorrow, the day after," Louie said.

"Ask him whatever happened to Joe Brusher. You ask him that for me, all right? You remember, or maybe you wanna write it down, or what?"

"I got it."

Il Capraio nodded vaguely, then turned his eyes toward the line of another dim horizon. Louie and the old man listened to his receding footsteps and watched his back as he walked away and out into the wayward springtime breeze.

"I came, I saw, I conquered," the old man said. In his voice, there was more resignation than contempt.

Softly, drops of rain began to fall against the window, streaming down in windblown tendrils of wet refraction; and there was thunder. Louie lighted another cigarette and wondered.

Sitting at her drafting table, laying down pale blue bleed-lines on a fresh illustration board and nibbling with her teeth at the skin of her lips, Donna Louise Craven listened to the quiet young stranger in the cubbyhole across the way. He was talking on the telephone, saying "I love you, too." Donna glanced at him and smiled.

She waited until everyone around her had ambled out to lunch, then she lowered her T-square, wiped out her ruling pen, and looked at the telephone on the little wooden cabinet beside her. Uttering a throaty sound halfway between exasperation and abandon, she lifted the receiver and dialed. Her left hand closed tight on the arm of her chair as she listened to the ringing at the other end. Then Louie answered, and she raised her left hand to her throat.

"It's me," she said, smiling uneasily.

"And how are you, Donna Lou?" His voice sounded good to her.

"Oh, I miss you, Louie," she said, not really meaning to say it, starting to laugh and very nearly crying. "It's been awhile."

"Tell me about it. If the new issue of *Leg Art* doesn't come out soon, I'm gonna start contemplatin' the gay life."

She began to smile easily now. "That's one thing you never had trouble with, Louie, finding women."

"I ain't been with anybody since I been with you."

"Oh, Louie, you lie like a rug." She laughed.

Then there was silence. Louie could hear Donna Lou breathing through her nostrils.

"What do you think, Louie?" she sighed.

"What do I think?" he said calmly but in a voice that no longer sounded good to her. "You put me through nine kinds of hell, leave me standin' here with my dick in my hand, disappear for two months, then call up out of the blue and say 'What do you think?' You know what I think? I think you must have balls made out of solid brass." He was sitting in his skivvy shirt and boxer shorts, and when he said this he reached down and scratched his own.

"Oh, Louie, I don't know."

"You never did, if that means a fuckin' thing to you." He heard her breathe again, and he thought again of her hair in his hand, and those golden spitcurls above her cunt, and her legs in nylon, and the line of her neck; and he lowered his voice again. "Why don't you come on over later."

There was the space of a breath before she spoke: "I think I'm coming down with a cold or something."

"I got tea. I got honey. I got lemons. We'll play doctor."

"I'd like that."

"The doctor'd like it, too."

"I love you, Louie." She said this as if stating a sad but ineluctable fact.

Louie heard the need in her voice, and, in that part of his mind from which no good came, he relished it. But he found himself saying "I love you, too," and meaning it more than he ever thought he could.

Louie hung up the receiver and shook his head. Uncle John was right: It moved mountains, that thing down there between their legs.

He stood in his underwear and looked at himself in the mirror. He recalled the old days, not really so long ago, when he could cause the lips of women to quiver merely by looking in their eyes, and could see in those eyes the dumb, hungry illusion that perceived him as something dangerous and desired and hard. By the time he had turned eighteen, he knew that he could have them all; and for a long while that had been true. But those days were over. He stared into his own sea-colored eyes, seeing the lines beneath them and the creases above his brow, and the brown hairs that bared more of his temples than they once had done. He looked at his scars, the one on the chin that had been stitched neatly by an emergency-room intern, and the one near his left eye that had been left to heal itself because he had chosen not to leave the bar and go to the hospital with the others who had been hurt in the same meaningless fight. He stroked them lightly with his finger: cheap mementos of the days when he believed he was tough, the days when he often doubted that he would live to see thirty-five. Yet here he was, staring at it face to face.

He made a fist and bent his arm. His biceps still looked good, even though he had not done a pushup so far this year. He slapped his gut, shaking his head in subdued disgust. If he had all the money he had spent while drunk, he would be able to buy a house, he reflected. Instead, he had bought this. He sucked his belly in, beginning to see in the mirror the image of himself as he was ten years ago and more. Then, as a dull pain in the small of his back shot around his left hip, he eased his stance. He went to the kitchen, where his ledger lay open on the table.

He inhaled deeply and drummed upon the table with the eraser-tip of his pencil, looking down at what he now knew to be the arithmetic of futility.

It was supposed to have been so easy. Put out on the street in small loans on the twenty-week payment system at thirty percent, Louie's initial five grand should have increased in five months' time to $6,500. Put back out on the street in the same way, this was to have grown into $8,450 after another five months, then into $10,985, and so on. After two years and a month, his original five grand should have become $18,564. Relinquishing half his profits, $6,782, to the man in the dead man's polyester (and the propriety of this had been impressed on him early in his venture, when two gleaming black Cadillacs veered suddenly to the curb near where he walked, and a large stranger in a silvery silk suit loomed forth from one of the cars to say, "He's got you clocked, kid") would have left him with more than eleven grand, enough for him to begin making bigger, point-system loans. This was where his fortune was to have been made. Ten grand put out on the street in five-point loans would grow to $36,000 in a year. Put back out on the street in more five-point loans, this $36,000 would increase to $129,600 in another year's time.

Louie looked over the old calculations, grinning sardonically at their cocksure exactitude and marveling at his own innocence. He shook his head when he came to the place in his computations where he was to have become a millionaire:

$$
\begin{array}{rl}
\$\ \ \ 466{,}560 & principal \\
\times \ \ \ \ \ \ \ .05 & point\ rate \\
\hline
\$\ \ \ \ 23{,}328 & weekly\ vig \\
\times \ \ \ \ \ \ \ \ 52 & weeks \\
\hline
\$1{,}213{,}056 & profit \\
+\ \ 466{,}560 & principal \\
\hline
\$1{,}679{,}616 & gross
\end{array}
$$

Beneath this was a note that, at the prime, three-point rate, this $1,679,616 would grow to $4,349,816.96 in the span of a year.

"And ninety-six cents," he mumbled. He calmly tore the page from the book and dropped it in the wastebasket.

More than four years had passed since Louie had reckoned those figures. According to them, he now should have been closing in on his first half million. In fact, he had not quite twelve grand to his name, and most of that was out on the street. He knew more now about certain things than he did four years ago: about men who borrowed from Peter to pay Paul, men who got fired seven weeks into a twenty-week payment schedule, men who would tear out their own livers if there were a vital-organs window at Belmont, men with sick wives and no insurance, men who went to jail, men who cried, and men who died.

He knew that he should not complain, really. He had, after all, been able to quit working for Giacomo two years ago, and there were no hungry days. But he also knew that his fortune lay elsewhere, if it lay anywhere at all; and he spent as much time grasping in the vagueness for a scheme as he spent making the rounds and doing his books. The possibilities of errant fate beguiled and haunted him, and he sometimes became lost in them, like the blond waves and ambivalent flesh of Donna Lou, like the ghostly sighs of light from long ago, aswirl in the morning motes.

Joe Brusher taped a sterile pad above each of his heels, where the new extra-wide wing-tip brogues he had bought through the mail from the Big Man Shop had blistered his Achilles' tendons.

He pulled up his brown woolen socks, then eased into a well-worn pair of tennis shoes. He stood and ran his thumbs around the inside waistband of his neatly pressed beige slacks. He fastened two of the three buttons at the neck of his blue knit pullover, then put on a dark brown blazer. Turning to face the mirror, he carefully arranged his shirt collar so that it unfurled onto the lapels of his blazer. He walked to the little table near the door, where there was a ceramic swan on a crocheted doily. From the concave tray of the swan's back, he took two sets of keys, his billfold, three quarters, and his gold Rolex watch. As he slipped the watch on, he looked at the little chips of faded blue paint that were all that remained of the swan's eyes.

He opened the drawer at the end of the table and removed a gun, a Charter Arms 79K .32 with a cracked grip and threaded bushing. Reaching farther into the drawer, past pieces of paper, pens, and an old address book, he took out a Dater steel-and-aluminum silencer and screwed it onto the gun's bushing. He thumbed the safety and placed the gun inside his blazer, in the deep pocket near his left breast. He stood by the door for a moment as if immersed in thought; then he walked into the bathroom and pissed.

He locked up, walked the three flights down to the street, got in his maroon Buick, and drove.

As he emerged from the darkness of the Holland Tunnel into the falling afternoon light, he looked at his watch and noted with satisfaction that he had made good time. He steered his Buick up Hudson Street. When he came to the northwest corner of Vestry Street, he pulled up by the fire-plug there. Taking one of the quarters from his pocket, he stepped out to the pay phone.

"You ready, Harry? All right, listen. It's five after three. Meet me at three thirty. On Renwick Street, the garage where they used to stash the swag from Pier Forty."

He returned to the maroon Buick and drove to Canal Street. He turned left on Canal, then right on Greenwich, right on Spring, and finally right again on Renwick. He parked near the chain-link fence in front of the garage lot. He locked the car and unlocked the gate. He looked around.

The street—more of an alley, really, a cobblestone trough, steeped and stained with fifty years' spilled gas, looked blindly down upon by haunted cast-iron facades that had been dark for as long as Joe Brusher could re-member—was quiet and strewn with debris. Sheets of old newspaper and damp cardboard crating stirred and flapped faintly in the sad spring breeze.

He left the gate ajar and walked across what had been a small parking yard, now all cracked concrete and pale weeds and broken glass. He stepped onto the platform of the garage. With another key he unlocked the roll-up door. Raising the rusted door with some difficulty, he entered the garage. It was empty but for some piles of rags, a few wooden pallets and milk crates, a motor-oil can, and some beer bottles.

He dragged one of the milk crates to the threshold of the garage, to where the late afternoon light just barely reached. He put another crate between it and the wall, placing it a few inches farther back into the shadows. He sat on the outside crate. He adjusted the creases of his slacks and looked at his watch. It was twenty minutes after three. He reached into his blazer and released the safety catch.

The man whose name was Harry pulled up and parked his silver Buick behind Joe Brusher's maroon Buick.

"This place brings back memories," he said, closing the gate behind him. He was a little man with a dark tan, a thin gray mustache and curly gray hair, and he smiled as he walked.

"That's what I was sittin' here thinkin'," Joe Brusher said.

"Last time I seen this garage it was full of King Oscar sardines. Remember that? We must've hit every deli in New York tryin' to unload them damn sardines."

"Yeah. The good old days."

"So, this shit is good?"

"I don't know, Harry. I don't like to bullshit anybody, you know? I could pull your prick and tell you it's white death, but I don't do that. This stuff, I wouldn't be surprised the assholes that use it end up shittin' themselves to death, it's probably got so much of that *sicilian'* mannitol shit in it. On the other hand, they tell me it's as good as anything out there these days. What do you want for ten grand, anyway? This ain't the fuckin' French Connection."

"I can lay down my lantern," Harry said, smiling. "I have found an honest man."

"Yeah, whatever."

Harry sat on the vacant crate. "I'm gettin' old," he said. He turned to Joe. "How you feelin' these days?"

"I tell you my troubles, I'll only have to listen to yours."

"I hear you." Harry nodded. "So, what do you say

we take care of business and get out of this shit-hole?"

"Here."

Harry put out his right palm to receive the package, and in that instant he saw that it was not a package. The bullet bore into the skull beneath the terror in Harry's right eye, which filled with blood as his head snapped back against the wall and one hand jerked up toward the cruel hole that was the end of his life; and Joe Brusher, feeling the recoil reach his elbow, seeing the little drops of blood spatter his hand like rain, fired again into the head and wrenched loose the little man's soul.

He thumbed the safety of the gun, returned it to his pocket, then turned to the pockets of the dead man. He rose with two sheaves of bills bound by rubber bands. He riffled them and saw that they were all hundreds.

He rolled down the garage door and locked it, walked through the gate and locked it. He got into his maroon Buick. He put the gun and the money under the seat. From the glove compartment he took a Handi-Wipe and washed the blood from his wrist and fingers. Then he drove back through the Holland Tunnel to Jersey City, glancing at his watch and noting with satisfaction that he had made good time.

There was no tea that night, no honey and lemon. Donna Lou's skirt and blouse and camisole lay over the arm of the couch.

She touched her fingers to his arm and said nothing as he loosed the clasp between her breasts and let her flesh sigh forward. The rosy dappled skin round her nipples, then the pretty nipples themselves, stirred and stiffened as if caressed by somewhere's salt-sea breeze.

Her head lolled back into his waiting hand. He saw her nostrils flare, and he lowered his mouth to hers, slaking his tongue beneath hers and drawing her sweet breath into him, feeling her limbs loosen.

He pulled down her brassiere from behind. It fell to her elbows, then to the floor. He grasped her hip, the glorious inflection of her haunch, then let his fingers follow the lacy line of her panties, round the back of her soft thigh to the warm cusp between her legs. Her buttocks squeezed upon his hand, and she then drew his breath into her, undulating against him as the susurrus of that breath grew more wicked, until it was like the sound of a distant ocean, strength itself, and all weakness, too; and her eyelids were neither open nor closed, and she felt the weight and sinews of his cock, cruel and begging, against her; and her belly fluttered.

He clutched through her panties at the flesh and summery wetness and cornsilk curls, feeling the lips of her cunt swell and pout and liquiesce with the feverish magic of want. She lowered her open mouth to his neck and pressed her teeth to him. His cock twitched in slow violence on her belly. He raked his fingers through her blond waves, then tightened his grip and drew her away from him. He freed his cock from his shorts, and she put her cool, slender fingers to it, lightly; then clenched and brought her mouth again to his. He gathered the waist of her panties in his fist and drew her to the bed. She fell back onto it, and he pulled down her panties with both hands, tossing them to her face. She shook them away, sighing, opening her eyes and seeing him, naked, hunkering beside her, then straddling her.

She felt his cock against her breasts, her neck, her face. Her mouth opened slowly, seeking it. She drew it into her mouth, and he moaned, feeling the hollows of her cheeks with his fingertips as she sucked. He slapped her gently. Her mouth relaxed, and her tongue began to stir, slavering and laving and sensing every vein of his cock, as the power that existed between them, their souls' mystery, drifted and shifted from the one to the other. As her head moved, casting cobra shadows on the dim wall, drawing the power from him, giving it back to him, she lowered her hand to her cunt, moving her fingers softly, then wildly, maddening the tiny pink conundrum there, feeling the contractions and palpitations within her. Her head fell still, and her cheeks hollowed again, sucking, and her body was taut and vibrant and rapt, and it seemed to her that her hand would burst into flame.

He pulled his cock from her mouth and drew it down the length of her body; and her beautiful legs widened. Pinning her wrists to the bed, he slipped ever so slightly into her, bowed his head and took her breast in his mouth; then lunged into all of her. She gasped and furled her lithe legs around him, feeling the breath swell deep in her as he struck and rolled his hips against the drenched flesh of her crotch, seeming to glance her farthest, hungriest place.

She felt their skins burning together; and he, clutching her breast ravenously in his hand, groaned and burst, flinching, inside her; and her own fierce breath was released. And as she clung to him, and he to her, and her body and soul descended into that warm baptismal shoal, she realized that it felt as if it were the last time; and she prayed to God that it was not.

Drifting, she heard his voice, soft and low and as if far away, asking how she was; and she heard her own voice, far away, too, and sweeter than she knew it to be: "Baby, I could die."

When she was asleep, Louie rose and sat in the darkness. Entering his own shadow, he pondered the presence of Donna Lou in his bed. Only in the last few days had he begun to breathe full without her, had he begun to weld his desire for her and his loss of her into an armature within him. Now her breath had entered his own again, and the solder of that armature had melted and escaped through his cock. His happiness and his weakness, his blessing and his curse had returned and lay sleeping in his bed. He did not know whether to thank God or spit.

Joe Brusher and the one called Il Capraio sat at a table in the black-curtained room in the middle of the night.

"That little *genoese* prick," Il Capraio said. "That cocksucker."

"I'm lucky I ain't layin' up on First Avenue here. The little *chiacchieron'* wanted to talk about fuckin' old times first. A forty-five, no less. A goddamn fuckin' cannon, one of them Argentine things. No mixer, no nothin'. When the fuck did he start playin' with guns, the little prick?"

"You take it?"

"I left it on him. That way, the bulls find him, they can pull that 'mob-style rubout' routine without gettin' bent outa shape and havin' to miss happy hour at Tom O'Reilly's and all that shit. If they ever find him, that is. Who owns that fuckin' garage these days, anyway?"

"Lefty's kid, the one that takes it up the ass," Il Capraio said distractedly. "He don't come around no more since the old man died." He stood and walked to the window, parting the curtain and glancing out into the darkness. "I just can't figure it. He was a fuckin' pussycat, that little prick."

"Pussycats go crazy, too. And sometimes they bite."

"You checked the car and everything, huh?"

"Everything. He had thirty-somethin' bucks on him. And a fuckin' cannon. I didn't look up his asshole, but I figure it's pretty hard to fit ten grand in somebody's heinie."

"Still, it don't figure."

"What figures, Frank, is that he figured him and me were the only two people that knew him and me were gonna meet, and he figured fuck me. That's what figures. And, with all due respect to you, Frank, I don't need shit like that."

"I know, I know. Enough, hey?"

Joe Brusher walked to the small bar at the side of the room. He took one of the eight-ounce highball glasses from the drainboard, held it to the light, and slowly turned it. He looked for a moment at the dozen or so bottles behind the bar, and reached for the J & B. He poured some, then carried the drink back to the table where Il Capraio sat in silence. From his jacket he took a small plastic vial, removed its cap, and shook a small white pill into his hand. He placed the pill in his mouth and washed it down with some of the Scotch.

"You sleepin' these days, Joe?"

"Ah"—he shook his head—"I close my eyes, you know? Forty winks here, forty winks there." He sipped his drink. "I take the Valiums. Now the doctor gave me this new shit, Elavils, whatever the fuck they are. I was never much of a sleeper, you know that."

Il Capraio slowly nodded. Through the breach in the curtains, he saw the figure of Giacomo pass slowly by on his way to open his store. Seeing the light, he nodded stonily toward the illuminated slit between the curtains. Il Capraio shook his head. "Another fuckin' *pazzo*. Twenty years in the can, one foot in the grave, nickel-and-dimin' it all the way." He inhaled deeply, then looked at the clock. It was three thirty.

"I don't know, Frank," Joe Brusher said after a while. "You know? I mean, who needs this shit?" He sipped, then he breathed. "I watch the TV. They got one guy, some half-a-fruit, shootin' the other guy, and they got the music in the background, and next thing, the guy who shot the other guy is out on the veranda there drinkin' Châteauneuf-du-Piss with some broad who's smackin' her chops and lookin' at him like he's Christ with a hard-on. Shit. Last time I got laid, it cost me a hundred bucks." He swallowed the last of the liquor and pushed the glass away. "And I never heard none of that music in the background, you know what I mean?

"Shit. I'm just workin' on gettin' my forty acres and a mule, and that's it. You got any idea what I went through drinkin' and gamblin' when I was young? Forget it! I really believe, Frank, as God is my witness, I am the stupidest fuck I ever met. I mean that." He shrugged and gesticulated abstrusely with his right hand. "Then again, at least I'm still here." He gesticulated again and nodded in corroboration of his own words. "I never really regretted, you know, the things I did to make money. I never did. That time that Chink, whatever the fuck he was, who should've been ironin' shirts somewhere or passin' out fortune cookies instead of playin' doctor, fucked up that gallbladder operation on me up at Lenox Hill there and I nearly croaked, they had the priest in there with me and he's lookin' like, hey, this is a job for the exorcist, and my fat-ass sister is starin' at me tryin' to figure out where she should start crowbarrin' up the floorboards in my apartment; even then, dyin' and doped-up and spooked as I was, I didn't feel sorry for a fuckin' thing. Just what I done with the money after I got it." He fell quiet. "Jesus, I think these elevator pills make you talk a lot."

Il Capraio was still gazing at the part in the curtains. He looked as if he had not heard a word of what Joe Brusher had said. The room was so silent now that the electrical hum of the fluorescent lamp could be heard. Il Capraio steepled his fingers upon his chest.

"You see Giovanni Brunellesches lately?" he said.

Joe Brusher shook his head.

"He don't get around much anymore, Frank. He's gotta be pushin' eighty now, for Christ's sake. I don't think he's been doin' anything since they put away that guinea mayor there, that Addonizio."

"He's doin' somethin', all right. I don't know exactly what it is, but he's doin' it. It's got to have somethin' to do with those *tizzunes* out there."

"What are you sayin', Frank?"

"The numbers, Joe, the numbers. Newark used to be good for about two hundred grand a day in numbers. Now they got the legal numbers in Jersey, just like here; you know that. And there they sell the legal numbers in liquor stores and all. The State cut into the action out there a lot worse than here. But it still don't make sense that Newark should go from two hundred grand a day to—you got any idea what it is these days, Joe? I know what it is, Joe, 'cause every afternoon all the action here and most of Jersey ends up in the kitchen of a house in Hackensack, and all that action gets tallied and divvied accordingly; and my guy, who's out there every day for that tallyin' and divvyin', told me what Newark brings in these days, and what Newark brings in these days is about twenty grand a day. From two hundred K to twenty K a day, in the *tizzune* capital of the world. Even if the State was givin' out free watermelon and wine with those legal numbers, it still wouldn't make sense, a drop like that. Nobody could figure it. Then somebody said somethin'—it was you, Joe, you said somethin' about the old Harlem numbers. I started to think. He sits out there, nobody hears from him, nobody bothers him. Hey."

"He's an old-timer like you, Frank. He's been around, from what I hear."

Il Capraio remembered a snowy day a long time ago, and a basement beneath what was now a joint called Vincent's, ten blocks or so from where he now sat. He remembered the Coke bottles of wine and the bowls of *capozelle* and Giovanni's voice, all still clear in his mind after half a century and more. And just as clear was the hatred he had felt then, as a boy of barely seventeen, for that boy of twenty-two who had all the ideas and all the balls and all the style. And he remembered the sweetest day of his youth, the day when Frank Costello patted his cheek and said, *"Mio figlio, mio bravo figlio."*

"Yeah, he's an old-timer, all right. But times change." Il Capraio rubbed his temples. "Besides, he's a fuckin' *albanese.*"

"He's Albanian? I thought he was born in Italy, that he was *pugliese* or some shit."

"Yeah, sure, he was born in Italy, but he's still *albanese*; his blood's *albanese*. What do you think that name is? That ain't no Italian name; it's a nanny-goat version of one of them *albanese* names. And I never trust a fuckin' *albanese.*"

Joe Brusher said nothing. Il Capraio crossed his legs loosely, then wiped with his longest finger at the corner of one eye. "Anyway, I figured I'd throw a scare into him. He's got this nephew around here, some two-bit shylock or whatever the fuck he is this week. He goes out to see him pretty regular. I told him to ask him whatever happened to Joe Brusher. I figured that might remind him he's bein' thought of on this side of the river."

"Frank, with all due respect—and I don't give a fuck one way or the other about the bastard; he's nothin' to me— but wouldn't it make sense to just let the guy fade away in peace?"

"Joe, you don't see. If he's got somethin' goin' with those *tizzunes* and he does fade away, there'd be no correctin' the situation. There'd be no takin' hold of those *tizzunes*. They'd just keep on doin' without him what they're doin' with him; it'd be lost forever. Without him, where would you begin to figure out what was goin' on over there? You could burn down the Sixth Ward and half of Broad Street, and you still might only be gettin' warm. No, he's gotta be the one to correct the situation, or at least explain it. Then he can fade away, maybe whether he wants to or not."

"Frank, you're a smart man."

Il Capraio shrugged in a grotesque expression of modesty. The two men sat there, leaning against the wall, still as a frieze.

"Do you think, Frank, I could put the touch on you for some walkin'-around money till the weekend? Half a hundred, say?"

Il Capraio withdrew money from his pocket. He snapped free two twenties and a ten, placed them in front of Joe Brusher, then waved the back of his hand at them. Joe Brusher thanked him.

"Have another one," Il Capraio said, tossing his index finger toward the empty glass. Joe Brusher shook his head. "Then wash the glass," Il Capraio said.

Louie emerged from Penn Station into the sunshine and squalor of downtown Newark.

He walked up Raymond Boulevard to Broad Street. Crossing through Military Park, he saw a black man in splayed, laceless boots and a ragged topcoat wrenching newly bloomed tulips from their bed and throwing them violently to the pavement.

"Don't you look at me like that, white man," the black man exclaimed. "I know that look. I don't like that look."

"Fuck you," Louie said casually, walking on. The black man humphed, then returned to his mission.

Louie turned the corner to Halsey Street. On a folding chair near the door of the narrow building where his uncle lived, there sat a heavyset black man in a white windbreaker and a black homburg. A long hardwood shillelagh leaned against the wall close by.

"Hello, Ernie."

The heavyset man turned toward the voice. He saw Louie and broke into a broad smile. "Louis," he said.

A group of young black boys passed. One of them carried a suitcase radio that blared distortion. Another of them danced along spasmodically while blowing large pink bubbles.

"I sit here and I look around," Ernie said as the blare died away, "and I think of what Newark was like years ago. It was some kind of town. You ever see an after-hours joint with a maître d'?"

"Never," Louie laughed.

"Yeah, well, someday you ask your uncle about Henry Meyer's place." He pulled a Partagas cigar from his breast pocket, removed it from its copper-colored metal tube, and carefully snipped its rounded end with his teeth. "Newark made New York look like a Methodist tank town." He struck a match, held it to the cigar, then puffed. "Ah, well, like your uncle used to say, as goes Newark, so goes the world."

"How is he?"

"Rock of Gibraltar." Ernie smiled. "We walked down to the bar the other day. He had his few. Every year, same thing. He starts in talkin' 'bout those barrels of bock beer the bars used to get in the springtime; then it's 'What do you say we go down for a cold one?' He's still got that bottle of brandy up there. A shot in the morning, maybe one at night." Ernie tapped an ash onto the sidewalk. "Yesterday I went with him to get his hair cut." Ernie laughed a little. "You ever see that barber he goes to over there on New Street? I think he's older than your uncle. Holds the damn scissors with two hands." Then Ernie blew smoke, and he seemed to think awhile, and the smile faded from his face. He looked into the younger man's eyes. "There is somethin', Lou," he said. "You ever known your uncle to use a telephone?"

"Are you kiddin', Ernie. Forget about it." Louie shook his head. "When I was a kid, my old man told me that when he was a kid, when they were all livin' together— my great-grandfather and great-grandmother, my grandfather and grandmother, all the brothers—in the house in Jersey City, my grandmother wanted a telephone. My grandfather wouldn't allow it to be listed in his name. It had to be listed in hers. And they never went near that phone, either Uncle John or my grandfather. If it rang and there was no one home but them, they just let it ring. They wouldn't even look at it except to curse it.

"I remember one time, Uncle John came home with my grandfather after visiting Mayor Gangemi or one of those guys. I asked him what the mayor's house was like, and all he said was, 'He had two phones.' It was like he'd caught the guy wearin' women's underwear or somethin'."

Ernie was silent for a moment, and he looked away before he spoke again. "Well, I'll tell you something. A few weeks ago, he had a couple of the guys from Local 827 come by and put in a phone. You believe that? And he keeps lookin' at it, like he's waitin' for it to ring."

Louie looked at Ernie and uttered a low sound of dismay, which Ernie could not hear.

"And there's somethin' else," Ernie said. "He sent off to the Justice Department in New York for a copy of his citizenship papers. Then he had me take him to the camera shop over there on Park Place to get his picture taken." He tapped more ashes onto the pavement; then he looked quizzically at Louie. "It was for a passport," he said. "He upped and got himself a damn passport."

The two men looked at each other; then Louie patted Ernie on the shoulder. "Let me go up and see him," he said. "I'll catch you later."

He unlocked the front door with a key from his pocket, and he entered.

He had known the inside of this building since he was a child. He had climbed the stairs to his uncle's rooms countless times with his father, and with other uncles; then countless times alone. As a boy, passing from the minatory din of downtown Newark into the sudden quietude of this vestibule, he always had felt as if he were entering a sanctuary, so remarkable was the contrast between the tumult on the one side of the great steeled oak door, the silence on the other. It was as if that door shut out more than the troublesome streets. It was as if it shut out the world and time itself.

Louie glanced at the little painting in the pine-molding frame that hung at the foot of the stairs: a view of foreboding trees beyond a gloomy lake. Over the years, Louie had seen the little painting slowly darken with age till, now, it seemed not a picture of trees and water at all, but only of foreboding and gloom. He laid his hand on the dark-varnished banister, and he ascended the creaking stairs to the second floor, every creak seeming, now as forever past, to summon forth from the stillness of this sanctuary shades of the dead, and to stir within himself some vague undying thing that felt, at times, like power.

The creaking ceased. He rapped lightly on the door, and he heard the old man's shuffling steps, as slow and regular as a sleeping heart.

"Hello, stranger," the old man said.

Louie followed his uncle to the easy chairs by the window. As he moved, the old man maneuvered his suspenders onto his shoulders. Slowing his pace so as to keep behind him, Louie glanced around. The window was closed, as usual, just as, Louie knew, the windows in the kitchen and the bedroom were open, as usual. The lace curtains transmuted the streaming sunshine into soft, delicate rays, which purled like churchlight on the room's familiar furnishings and pale blue walls. Like all but one of the old man's walls, these were bare. Only above the head of his bed was there any graven image of anything or anyone: a heavy bronze crucifix, adorned year-round with the woven palm leaf that Louie brought him during the last week of every Lent. The old man's cane was propped against the mahogany end table between the two easy chairs. His tweed cap was on the table. A magnifying glass lay on a folded copy of the day's *Star-Ledger*. There were White Owl cigars in cellophane wrappers, and a box of De Nobilis, but the big crystal ashtray was clean. And, yes, there was that thing, the last thing that Louie would ever have expected to see atop this table: a shining black telephone.

They sat. The old man adjusted his hearing aid, then offered Louie a cigar, as he always did. Louie declined, as he always did, and lighted a cigarette.

"New haircut," the old man said happily, gesturing toward his head.

"Yeah. Ernie told me." Louie smiled, looking at the thick silver hair that had defied all aging for the last twenty years, then at the face below it, the face of his kindred blood.

"New slippers," the old man said, pointing to his feet. Louie looked down at the fancy slippers of soft brown leather, and he grinned, so incongruous were they with the old man's shabby gabardine trousers and plaid flannel shirt. "Every time I see you," the old man smiled, "you ask me what's new. I figured I'd beat you to the punch today." And they both laughed without making a sound, beholding each other in the churchlight.

"Somethin' else new, too," Louie said slyly. He tilted his head toward that black plastic improbability.

Uncle John neither spoke nor smiled then. His face relaxed into the vague, inscrutable frown of age, but Louie saw the flicker of censure behind the old man's spectacles. Then the laconic frown turned upward into the semblance of a grin.

"Phone sex," the old man said solemnly. "They got that now. You call up and you pay and the woman talks to you. They had all about it on 'Donahue' the other day. Imagine payin' a woman to talk? That's like payin' a bird to fly." He took his glasses off and rubbed them with his handkerchief. "Imagine payin' *anybody* to talk," he said quietly. Then he looked sternly into Louie's eyes. "So, how have you been, kid?"

"Good," Louie said, indecisively.

Uncle John nodded, grimacing in approval. "Next time I see you, you'll bring the palm." It was neither a question nor a statement, really, but more of an oblique musing on the passing cadences of time. "Then, the week after that, baseball." He gestured toward the dead television set across the room. "Maybe I'll go with the Mets again this year. What do you think?"

"They got a shot."

The old man nodded very slowly, and he looked blankly through the delicate rays. He sat in this manner, breathing softly, peering abstractedly, as if he were alone, not only in this room but in this world as well. When, at last, he slowly nodded once again, it seemed that he was signaling his assent to some impalpable sovereignty beyond the slivered light, or merely acknowledging those shards of himself that through the years had been lost to the rayless drift. Then he turned to Louie as if to say: I'm still here, and you're here with me. They grinned softly at the absurdity of fate that had cast them together, two stubborn links from a shattered chain.

"You ever think of settling down and having kids?" the old man asked.

"Once in a while. How about you?" Louie watched the old man soundlessly laugh. "Why?"

"Because otherwise it ends with you. You're the last card in the boot. Granted, that doesn't mean much. Like just about everybody else in this world, we were only flies on history's back. Still, you get old, you think about these things. *L'ultimo di casa Brunellesches*," he said and grinned. "That's what you are. Unless you have a son."

"I think of it," Louie said, and he turned his hand nonchalantly.

"That's what I did. I thought about it. I'm still thinkin' about it," he laughed quietly. "That's one thing my brother Virgilio, your grandfather, did right. He got married young. Seemed like he shaved for the first time one day, got hitched the next. That's the way to do it, jump right in there before you know the score. Once you get used to going it alone, it's hard to give up the elbow room."

Louie breathed agreement through his nose. The old man fell still. Louie waited awhile and then asked: "Do you know a guy named Joe Brusher?"

The old man looked at him, and there was no smile. "Yeah," he said. "Do you?"

"No. But somebody asked me to ask you whatever happened to Joe Brusher."

The old man nodded sternly, as if there were something to accept in Louie's words. He closed his hand into a fist, and he beheld it, remembering the strength that once had lain therein. He unclenched it slowly before his eyes; then he lowered his hand calmly to the arm of his chair, braced himself, and slowly stood. He reached into his pocket and removed a dollar. He sat down and placed the bill on the end table, closer to Louie than to himself. "What is it, Louie?" he asked.

"It's a dollar bill," Louie said warily.

"Right. It's a piece of paper called a dollar. When I was a kid, a dollar bill represented a one-dollar gold piece. It was like that until the Depression. Then Roosevelt outlawed gold, and a dollar bill represented a silver dollar. It was called a Silver Certificate, and it said 'one silver dollar payable to the bearer on demand.' You remember those. Eventually, twenty years ago, they put an end to that, and a dollar note stopped representing anything: payable to the bearer on demand *un' gazz'*. But, yeah, for the sake of convenience, we'll call it a dollar bill.

"Now turn it over. See where it says 'In God We Trust'? That's something they added in the late fifties, when they were getting ready to renege on the 'payable to the bearer' bit. Look to the left there. What's that pyramid with the eye on it?"

Louie looked at it, that strange symbol that he had

looked at, without seeing, every day of his grown life; and he said he did not know.

"It's the reverse of the Seal of the United States, and the back of the dollar is the only place you'll ever see it. It's Mason horseshit. The people that started this country— Benjamin Franklin, Thomas Jefferson, Paul Revere—they were all Masons. And it was Masons who made that seal and passed it through Congress in the seventeen hundreds. Think about that sometime, Louie.

"But look at the words over the eye. What does it say there?"

Louie slowly pronounced the Latin words.

"That's no Mason mumbo-jumbo," the old man said. "They're about two thousand years old, those words. They were written by Virgil during the days of the first Roman emperor, Augustus. Augustus ran the first lottery in history."

The dollar-bill routine, Louie mused, was a new one. But now the old man had returned to familiar ground. He was on his Roman kick, Louie told himself; next stop, Albania. By now, Louie had ceased to wonder what all this had to do with the question that had brought it on. That question itself, along with the name of Joe Brusher, had faded from Louie's mind, swept away by the strange slow tide of his uncle's words.

"What Augustus started two thousand years ago was still going strong in Italy when I was born. They called it the Giuoco del Lotto. I've told you all about the Giuoco, Louie, and about the *albanese*, Il Santo, I worked for. We took bets all over the Lower East Side, everything from a penny to a dollar. Everybody, no matter how poor, had something to bet. They figured they couldn't go wrong for a penny or a nickel or a dime. We must've handled more change in a week than the Federal Reserve Bank on Liberty Street.

"But, see, the thing was, those people who figured they couldn't go wrong for a penny or a nickel or a dime, they were going wrong. If they were lucky—and they all believed in luck more than they believed in anything; luck is the religion of failure—they stood to be paid off at a million to one. They thought that was great. But the real odds they were up against were almost forty-four million to one. It was a sucker's bet.

"I watched those people, day in and day out, and I took their money and I gave it to the Devil and the Devil gave me my pence. By the time I was twenty, I saw those people the way a whore sees a drunken sailor. Of course, I didn't think I was a whore. See, they've got bad names for women who sell flesh, but they don't have any for men who sell dreams."

Uncle John stopped for a minute, thinking back, almost receding into the shadows of those days. Then he turned to Louie. "I had hair just like you then," he said.

"Then all that shit happened. You know, Louie, they say you can't fight City Hall. And they're right. It's solid granite and marble." He looked through the lace; then his eyes rested on the rainbow in the prism of the crystal ashtray. "I think you know about that, Louie. I never told you, but I'm sure your father or somebody else did."

He did not look at Louie when he said this; he did not want him to feel as if he had to say anything. And Louie did not say anything, but he recalled a drunken argument he had overheard as a boy; recalled the bellowing voices of his father and Uncle John in the cellar, the slam of a fist on the table, then the constrained fury of his father's words: "What can you do about it? Kill them like you did those two fuckin' donkeys? Get locked up for another five years?" Louie remembered his mother, distraught, trying to call him away from the cellar stairs. It was the dead of summer.

"See, Louie, by 1930, the Giuoco was becoming a thing of the past. Uptown, Harlem had been running its own racket for years. At first, they had what they called Treasury tickets. In the early twenties, Treasury tickets gave way to what they called the clearing-house numbers. Everybody just called them 'the numbers.' You picked three digits. If they matched the last two figures in the millions of the exchange's total and the last figure in the millions of the balances announced that day by the New York Clearing House down on Nassau and Cedar, you got paid off at five hundred to one.

"These numbers became the biggest thing in New York. They spread everywhere, like fire, till there wasn't a city in the country without the numbers. It got so out of hand that the U.S. attorney—Roper was his name—strong-armed the newspapers into not printing the clearing-house figures in the financial pages. That was in the fall of '29, right around the time of the Crash. Soon after that, the New York Clearing House itself agreed to stop disclosing its figures. That's when the Harlem bosses switched to the Cincinnati Clearing House figures. There was no stopping the numbers.

"Il Santo had known about the Harlem numbers for a long time. He'd done a lot of business up there, in the Italian part of East Harlem, and that's where a lot of his *bub-bonia*, his dope, went. But he laughed at the numbers. *La Borsa negra*, he called them: the nigger stock exchange. Then it was too late, and he was too old to care.

"All he wanted was to go back to Italy and die in the little town where he was born. He still had people there. He used to talk about how when a man died there, the women laid him out and washed his body down with their tears and their hair, the old *albanese* way. So, that's what he wanted, to take his money and go like a lord to that town and sit in the sun and die in the shade and have those broads cry on his corpse. But it didn't happen that way.

"The few guys that were his partners were never what you'd call equal partners. He shared the Giuoco money, in his way, but the *bubbonia* money was always his alone. He wouldn't even tolerate talk of that money. And when he made up his mind to go back to the other side, he gave the Giuoco to his partners, but he said nothing about the heroin. Those men knew that the Giuoco was dying. And they knew that the heroin business was worth a fortune. They knew that as soon as Prohibition was over—and the writing was on the wall, it was only a matter of time—there'd be a mad scramble for the *bubbonia*. But Il Santo had someone, or something, other than them in mind for his operation. So they decided that the only way to take control was *la vuoda*. And that was the end of Il Santo: five in the head sitting at his kitchen table on the third day of September, 1930."

The old man paused and blew his nose into his plaid handkerchief. He asked Louie to bring him a glass of cold mineral water from the bottle in the refrigerator, and to get himself one, too. Louie did so, and the old man drank.

"Best drink in the world," he said. Then he breathed gravely and continued on.

"They threw the Giuoco to us like a bone. Me and three others. We were just punk kids, but we knew enough to bury that bone in Harlem.

"Downstairs at the corner of Mott and Hester, right where that shit joint, that Vincent's Clam Bar, came to be, there was an old *capozzell'* joint. They sold Coke bottles of wine for a dime, bowls of *capozzell'* for a buck. That's where I told the others how we could break the numbers without getting our shirts dirty.

"That was a little before Thanksgiving 1930. The next week, we took a train to Cincinnati and checked into a hotel. The Cincinnati Clearing House was on the fourth floor of the First National Bank Building at Fourth and Walnut. We went there and found the guy whose job it was to write the figures on the slate for the press each morning. His salary was something like fifty dollars a week. We offered him two grand to round off three digits to zeros. He didn't hesitate, not for a minute. We set the date for December eleventh. It was as easy as that.

"Two of us stayed there, in Cincinnati, and two of us came back to New York. There was a man named Castiglia who went by the name of Costello. We knew him through Il Santo. He was in the process of putting Tammany Hall into his back pocket. When you looked over this guy's shoulder, you didn't see six guineas from Thompson Street, you saw City Hall. So, we went to see him. I talked to him in Italian. He agreed to back us. He would put up the money for the clearing-house clerk, and he would put our bets, along with his own, straight into Harlem through his people—people that Miro and the other Harlem bosses wouldn't dare fool with.

"By three o'clock that Wednesday afternoon—December tenth—Harlem was holding more than five thousand dollars' worth of action on zero-zero-zero. There was a pawnshop up there called Blue White Diamonds, where you could lay a grand on a number and get paid off half a million in cash if you hit. At the end of that afternoon, Castiglia walked in there and laid down ten hundred-dollar bills. 'I had a dream,' he told the shine.

"The next day, there it was, over the wires and in the papers: zero-zero-zero. Harlem went crazy. Castiglia and his people got what money there was from the numbers banks, then they went to Blue White Diamonds for the rest. Miro and the other bosses were busted. One of them blew out his own brains, another left town. And Castiglia and his friends became the partners of those who remained. I figured I was one of those friends."

The old man lifted his glass in his left hand to drink, and Louie's eyes caught the familiar, august gleam of the big diamond ring that his uncle never removed. As a boy, when his family was poor, Louie had learned the meaning of *malocchio* by watching the eyes of his aunts as they gazed upon that stone.

"Castiglia gave me twenty grand. He told me there would be more. In the meantime, he wanted me to come up with a new numbers system, one that couldn't be rigged as easily as the clearing-house numbers.

"I gave it some thought and figured the last three digits of the New York Stock Exchange summary would be a good gimmick. And, for a while, it was. But after a few months, the board of directors of the exchange wised up and started substituting ciphers for the last three digits. It was almost as if, with the Depression and all, the exchange was worried about becoming a subsidiary of the numbers.

"That's when I came up with what came to be called the New York numbers. You took the payoff prices of the first three races at the track each afternoon and added them up. Say those eighteen prices totaled $91.50. Then you added on the payoff prices of the next two races. Say the new total was $192.00. Then you added on the payoff prices of the sixth and seventh races. Say you ended up with $415.20. You took the last digit before each of the three decimal points and put them together. Here it would be one-two-five. That was your number for the day."

Louie had grown up with people playing the numbers all around him, and he had been told by his grandfather that there would be no numbers, as people knew them, had it not been for Uncle John. He had believed this as a boy. Unaware that the numbers were illegal—even his first-grade teacher and the cop on the corner played them—he was sure that, when he was able to read books without pictures, he would find Uncle John's name written as bold in history as the names of Columbus and Einstein. But then, in adolescence, he had ceased believing it, and it became just another of the lies that died with his grandfather. After that, he had believed it and disbelieved it, until his father, not long before he died, denied the truth of it in a way that left no doubt in Louie's mind that it was true. Yet, until this moment, Uncle John himself had never broached the subject. Like most of what lay between them, it had been unspoken.

"It was a beautiful system," the old man reflected. "Later, they added the Brooklyn numbers. You just looked at the bottom of the racing charts in the paper each day and whatever the last three digits of the track handle were, that was the Brooklyn number. With two numbers, the New York and the Brooklyn, drawing action every day, and with both paying off at five hundred on a dollar, against real odds of nine hundred ninety-five to one, the racket was bringing in millions a week. Then they added the single action, sending runners out in the afternoon to take bets on the New York number one digit at a time, as it came out. They paid off seven to one, with real odds of nine to one; fifty-nine to one on what they called a bleeder, two digits bet at once.

"People were crazy for numbers. It was a disease. And, like every disease, it was a goldmine. But they don't give out copyrights in the rackets, and they don't pay royalties. That twenty grand I got didn't last too long. I bought myself a Packard coupe—a convertible. I bought this ring. I had a lady friend; I bought her a sable coat, and one day when I was drunk I paid off the mortgage on her mother's house in Brooklyn. A dime here, a grand there. Like they say, a fool and his money.

"So I went to see Castiglia. Was I not his friend? Of course I was. I reminded him of his promise, that there would be more money coming to me. I talked in Italian to him, and he answered me in Italian. *'E meglio il cuor felice che la borsa piena,'* he said. 'Better a happy heart than a full purse.' "

The old man drew breath.

"I thought awhile, then I drank awhile. Then I got some blood on my shirt, and that was that. The government took those five years from me. That was all right. I tacked them on to this end."

He pointed to the floor of the here and now.

"At that time, Louie, Sing Sing was a very bad place. I did nothing but sit in the dark for months. I smoked cigars and I spat and I thought the worst things a man can think. Then, one morning—it was this time of year; you could smell spring in the breeze from the river—I woke up and I was strong. I had caught that breeze.

"The way Sing Sing was set up at the time, the library was on the first level, in the open area where you came down to go into the yard. So, I walked in there that morning. The librarian was a faggot, a little guy from down South somewhere. They called him Betty Boop. He kept a box of old Kotex pads in his cell. 'Come by for a sniff,' he'd say. 'It's almost like bein' with a broad.' Eventually, he cut his own throat. They sewed it up, and he ripped it open again with his bare hands.

"Anyway, I walked in there, and I looked around. It wasn't much of a library. But, then again, Sing Sing was never known for its readers.

"I knew what I wanted, but not exactly. See, that breeze I had caught, Louie, was the first suspicion of truth. And the truth was that I was blind. All those years, from the time I went to work for Il Santo to when those big doors shut behind me, I'd looked down on the suckers who were my bread and butter. I'd looked down on them without seeing that my road ran parallel to theirs, and that it led to the same place. The difference between their end and mine was only the difference between a coffin made of pine and a coffin made of bronze. After all was said and done, I was just a fancier make of sucker than them. While I stuck it to them, somebody was sticking it to me. I knew all about the odds they were blind to, but I was blind to the odds that governed my own fate. I had fallen for the oldest sucker's game in the world: faith. I'd trusted somebody named Frankie Scarpa. And while I was talking Italian to Castiglia, Frankie Scarpa was talking English. Frankie Scarpa and Castiglia's friend Dutchie got the numbers, and I got *un' gazz'*. Then one day, Dutchie trusted, too. A guard showed me a *Mirror* with Dutchie's picture in it. He was lying in a pool of his own blood, just a few blocks from where we are now. And the day came when Castiglia trusted, too.

"See, it hadn't really sunk in yet that whenever a man talks about trust and honor, there's a good chance that if you look over your shoulder, you'll see a brass cock aimed right at your asshole. It's just like that dollar bill: They put "In God We Trust' on it one day, the next day it's worthless. I was blind to all that. I had figured out how to rig the numbers, but I didn't see that I was being rigged. I wasn't alone. That's what that place, Sing Sing, was full of, blind men.

"Anyway, Louie," he said, with force in his voice, "I was in Sing Sing five years, and I learned some things. I taught myself to read Latin, and I learned *potestas*—power, Louie —from men who knew it. From them, in their tongue. And I learned that those two words, *annuit coeptis*, on the back of that dollar bill, were from a prayer for *potestas*. I learned that that's what that dollar was.

"What I really learned, Louie, was that the ways of the world are ancient. Il Santo, Castiglia, all of them: they had done nothing that hadn't been done two thousand years before. The same holds for everybody. Any man who thinks he has a new idea is only a fool who hasn't been around.

Like the Jews said, 'The thing that has been, it is that which shall be; and that which is done is that which shall be done; and there is no new thing under the sun.' Understanding the truth of that can give a man the greatest edge in the world."

The old man looked into Louie's eyes, and he did not look away from them until his own failing sight had ascertained that there was light in them.

"I got out of that place in 1936, and I went my own way. I got involved in politics, if you want to call it that, with Frank Hague there in Jersey City, around the time of the '37 election. Eventually, I settled here. I did all right. I stayed my own man. I never started trouble, and I never ran from it. It's more than half a century since I caught that breeze, and you know, Louie, it just got stronger and sweeter with time.

"I watched what happened to the numbers. As I said, Dutchie got his. There's a big gray stone in the Gate of Heaven Cemetery with his name on it. In '39, Jimmy Hines, the Tammany Hall boss who was Castiglia's real partner in the numbers, got sent away by Dewey, who was another cocksucker. Things were shaken up for a while, and the numbers ended up in a lot of new hands. My old pal Frankie Scarpa got knocked down a few pegs. And they all just got greedier.

"That was their downfall. They came up with that cut-numbers shit figuring they'd increase their take by a good ten percent. Now certain numbers, they said—anything with a one in the middle; seven sixty-nine, which most of the dreambooks gave as the number of death; those three zeros—paid off at only four hundred on a dollar. But say a guy has been playing one seventeen for ten years. Now the runner comes to him and says that his number's cut and it won't pay five hundred on one anymore. I don't care how stupid that guy is, he's going to think. And that's why when the State decided to take over the numbers, all it had to do was pay off at five hundred on one across the board, no cut numbers. The man that advised the State to do it that way was a smart man." He grinned slyly. "Whoever he was."

Louie drank the last of his water, peering at the old man through the bottom of his raised glass.

"More than a few times in the forties and fifties, even since then, I was asked by certain men to come back into the numbers. They knew about those three zeros I told you about. But I turned them down. I knew the day was coming when the State would move in. And in your lifetime, Louie, you'll see the day when the State takes over the numbers completely. In Jersey, they've nearly done it already, and last year, in New York, the State took in close to half a billion in numbers action." He looked to Louie. "Fifteen percent of that went to what they call 'administration.'"

It seemed to Louie that his uncle savored the syllables of that last, droll word. Perhaps he was only slowing to the long pause that followed. Louie saw that there was actual weariness now in the old man's face.

"There are people, Louie, who believe I've held a grudge against the numbers since that touch of *la fede* sixty years ago." He slowly, sternly shook his head. "They don't know about that breeze, Louie. And they don't know me." He looked again at his nephew.

"And so now here we sit, Louie. We've never talked, you and me, of trusting each other, or love or honor or any of that *mut*." Louie had not heard the sound of that Albanian obscenity for years. "I'm an old man who's done all right, an old man who's spent most of what he made, but who caught a breeze and got to breathe it for longer than most men.

"And now you come and you say to me that somebody says to ask me whatever happened to Joe Brusher."

The old man nodded firmly, as he had done when Louie had first said those words and the sun washed brightly through the lace.

"And I know that the somebody you're speaking of is the man you pay your union dues to. I know he is one of the men who came up with that cut-numbers shit, and I know that he is one of those who believe that I have a grudge. He's a man as bad as Il Santo, but he lacks in the brains and in the balls. His name is Frankie Scarpa, and they call him Il Capraio.

"And Joe Brusher is a man who was born with the eyes of a corpse, and who kills men.

"It's not really a question, Louie, that your friend"—and he did savor that word—"is asking me. He knows as well as I do where Joe Brusher is. No, it's not a question. It's a threat. It means nothing to me. I'm not brave, but I don't scare, either. What means something to me is that he is low enough to send my own flesh and blood as an errand boy against me. I hope you think about that, Louie.

"Now get me a pen and paper from the kitchen."

Louie brought him what he wanted. The old man thanked him, then put the paper on the table and brought his left hand steadily down upon it. Lowering his face to within inches of it, he carefully wrote Joe Brusher's name, and below the name an address on Fairmount Avenue in Jersey City. Then he folded it and handed it to Louie.

"There," he said, his tired face smiling with a last glimmer of strength. "There's his answer."

They sat in silence while the room slowly darkened. Louie watched the old man peer into the drift, and, as he watched, he knew that what he saw was all that remained for him of a past that he alternately cherished and despised. The room grew darker still, and Louie rose to switch on the lamp. Light flooded the room, and the old man raised his head.

"So, what do you say, pal, we'll go with the Mets again?"

"Yeah," Louie said. "We'll go with the Mets."

They talked awhile more, about batting averages and artificial turf, beer and the weather. Louie offered to bring him *abbacchio*, a fresh-killed baby lamb, when he brought the palm next week. The old man wanted him to take a fifty-dollar bill for the lamb, but Louie would not have it.

"Keep it," he said. "Maybe there's something on the back you missed."

When they said good-bye, the old man reached up with one arm, and Louie bent to hug him.

The reflection of the lamplight on the windowpane was bright against the falling gloom of dusk. The old man looked out and watched Louie walk away through the long springtime shadows.

The old man turned. Glancing at a piece of paper from his pocket, he lifted the gleaming black receiver from its cradle, then dialed.

"Yeah," Joe Brusher said.

"The kid bought it," the old man said.

arly the next morning, Louie returned to the Street of Silence, and he drank his coffee and he smoked and he played his numbers.

The happiness boys, he saw, were now sober, though sickly. They sat crowded around the small Formica-topped table beneath the bare bulb. One of them held a large auto-body dent-slammer in both hands.

"All we need's the right sheet-metal screw," he said.

"I'm tellin' you," another said, "it ain't a lever lock. You need a tension wrench. You need somebody who knows how to use a tension wrench."

"I say this is a lot of fuckin' trouble to go through," the third said.

"We're talkin' about fifty grand worth of plastic nine-millimeters here, Glock Seventeens. That oughta be worth a little trouble," said the one who owed Louie money.

"Whatever. All I'm sayin' is there's gotta be an easier way."

Giacomo turned stiffly to stare at them; then he turned stiffly back and shook his head.

"You look like shit, kid," he muttered to Louie after a while.

Louie, in a friendly enough way, was about to tell the old man to go fuck himself, but he did not.

He knew he looked bad. He had barely slept the night

before, and that morning he had not bothered to shave. In his mind, he still saw his uncle peering toward where the darkness gathered, and he still heard his words. He had been taken aback to learn that Il Capraio and his uncle had harbored hate for each other for so many years. Both men had always given the impression that nothing but a vague and faded acquaintanceship connected them. But it was not this revelation that had ruined his sleep. What truly perplexed him was that this knowledge had remained hidden from him all his life, hidden from him by his only breathing blooded kin, the one man whom, because of that blood tie, he trusted. He cherished that trust, as he cherished what could not be banished of his love for Donna Louise. He cherished these things because they were what kept him from renouncing all trust and all love; they were the seawall. For as long as he could remember, he had known the faces of men that had been recast by, or born into, that renunciation, the faces of those who came through that creaking door by the black-curtained window nearby. For as long as he could remember, he had feared looking into the mirror someday and seeing one of those faces. Thinking about his uncle's secrecy had led him to realize how little he himself told his uncle, or anyone; and he had lain there last night, in the hour of the wolf, feeling the seawall crumble. At least, he told himself, he should have taken the half a yard for the lamb.

While Louie was drinking his third cup of coffee, Il Capraio entered, and the room fell still. One of the men at the table raised his hand in greeting, but Il Capraio did not allow himself to see that hand. He stood beside Louie, commented blankly on the niceness of the day, and with an abrupt wave declined Giacomo's dreary offer of coffee. He rubbed his face and he cleared his throat and he stood there.

Louie produced the folded piece of paper his uncle had

given him, and he handed it to Il Capraio. He watched Il Capraio stare at it for a moment, slowly apprehending what it was; then he watched his face tighten as he read it. Slowly, Il Capraio refolded the scrap, then with the fingers of his right hand crumpled it into a tiny ball. He tapped that tiny ball of paper several times on the bar, then, strangely nodding, dropped it into an ashtray. He looked at the door and he breathed; then he walked to the door and was gone.

Louie looked to Giacomo with his eyebrows raised, and Giacomo, his thin lips downward, looked at him.

"I won't even ask," the old man said. He took the ashtray and dumped it into the trash can beneath the bar.

Louie snorted and smiled slightly; then he stretched his arms, rose, and strode back to the little table. As he approached, the one who owed him money leaned back and worked his hand into his pocket. Grinning, he gave Louie four twenty-dollar bills. Louie, not grinning, put them in his pocket and turned to walk away.

"Hey, I get a deuce back, don't I?"

Louie looked and he saw that he was serious.

"Domani," Louie said, *"domani."*

Louie walked west to the IND subway station at Sixth Avenue and Spring Street, pausing along the way to buy a *Daily News.* Twenty minutes later, he tossed the *News* into the garbage on Forty-second Street. He came to an ugly red storefront where a dirty yellow plastic sign flashed the colors of Christmas and announced XXX∗PEEPS∗MAGS∗VIDEOS in buckled black letters. Of all Louie's stops, this was his favorite.

"Let's go, gents, pick 'em out and take 'em home, this ain't the Public Library," bellowed the fat man who stood on the raised platform behind the counter. Several of the men who were browsing, rapt, through magazines stepped obediently forward; and the cash register began to ring. Louie stood beside a well-dressed mantislike fellow who held a briefcase in one hand and with the other raised to the counter a copy of *She-Male Cum Eaters.*

"Is he back there?" Louie said. He glanced into the glass showcase beneath the counter, where, staring back at him, there was a rubber face with an open mouth and six inches of gullet attached by an electrical cord to a black battery-pack.

Louie moved slowly through the long, narrow store, letting his eyes roam. He walked past *Anal Lesbos* and *Bite My Tits*, past *Assfucked Virgins* and *Housewife Sluts*, *Roped & Reamed* and *Choked on Cock*. He passed through the chamber in the rear, which was dimmer and which smelled of Lysol. Rows of shut booths, from which drifted low mechanical whirrings and forlorn coughs, advertised *Barnyard Blowjobs* and *Chubbies in Chains*, *3-Way Kindergarten* and *Chicks with Dicks*. At the far wall, near a lone Joker Poker machine, there was a door. Louie backhanded a seven-rap tattoo on it, and there came a croaking response.

The small office-storeroom was as it always was: a shambles. Behind a beat-up steel-and-woodgrained desk sat a dumpy man of about forty. His ink-stained sleeves were rolled to his elbows and the hinges of his eyeglasses were wrapped with yellowing tape. A disorderly two-tiered filing-tray, an automatic quarter counter, a calculator, and a telephone crowded the desktop. A framed photograph of the dumpy man's dumpy wife and dumpy children stood partly obscured by three stacked copies of a videocassette titled *Cunt Crazy*. Behind the dumpy man, on a wall that was otherwise bare, there was a Chemical Bank calendar and a sign that said YA GOTTA PAY YOUR DUES. The word DUES was crossed out and the word JEWS was written under it.

"Good morning, Lord Goldstick," Louie said, but with only some of the spirited mock courtliness with which he usually delivered those words. He sat down on a rickety slat-seat chair near the desk.

"It would've been if the Black Hawks had won last night," Goldstick said. He reached into a drawer and gave Louie a thin bundle of money held together by a big paper clip. Louie counted it, four hundred and fifty dollars, then put it in his pocket.

"Three more weeks and we're even," Louie said, releasing the words slowly in one long, low breath.

"Ah," Goldstick groaned, his face contorting as if in reaction to some bitter black bile rising within him. "I'll never be even. I came out of my mother feet first, been runnin' ever since." He leaned back. "If the Lakers didn't come through for me over the weekend, you would've had to settle for a pound of flesh today."

"No credit cards and no flesh," Louie said. "Not from people with dicks, anyway."

"Speakin' of credit cards and dicks," Goldstick said, moving suddenly forward, grinning, reaching into another drawer. "Get a load of these." He handed Louie a folder, and Louie opened it.

There were a dozen or so letters. Most of them were neatly typed, a few were scrawled. Clipped to each letter was a check for five hundred dollars, payable to Dreams, Inc. Louie began to read one of the letters, written in a harsh vertical hand.

"Dear Sirs," it began. "I want a woman with black hair dressed in the clothes I sent seperate to rub herself between her legs—not showing 'It' but thru the slacks—and keep saying over and over like she is crazy I want you Harry oh Harry put it in me and have her lick her lips and rub her tits and move around like she is real hot and in the end say I love you Harry not him and then blow a kiss. Beside the black hair make her about thirty and the size of the clothes I sent you. Thank you very much. And please return the clothes after she wears them."

The letter bore the signature of a man not named Harry. Louie looked at Goldstick, then replaced the letter and began reading one that was typed.

"Dear Dreams, Inc.," it opened. "The scene I should like played out is one featuring a girl in her teens, of the grisette type but stylish; svelte, blond, pink nails and lips, subtle rouge and mascara. She wears a pink silk chemise, sheer black LeBourget pantyhose, and red leather pumps with four-inch heels.

"The scenario is as follows. The girl is standing, bent over, touching the toes of her shoes. The camera is at ground level. Slowly, her fingers move delicately up her legs. The camera, remaining at ground level, follows them upward. Her hands reach the chemise, raising it, baring her. Her fingers linger at her belly, her breasts. She removes her hands, letting the chemise fall to cover her again (in slow motion, if possible). She lies on the floor, lifting the chemise above her hips. The camera rises so that it now looks down on her. With her nails, she rips open the crotch of her pantyhose. Grasping with both hands, she tears the hole wide. She removes one of her shoes, brings it to her mouth and caresses it. She licks it, then sucks its heel while fondling herself. (The sound of this sucking should be quite audible.) She removes her other shoe and slowly inserts its heel into her vagina, moving it in and out, while still sucking. She does this until she climaxes. Then she starts to cry. She licks the tears that run down to her lips, smearing her makeup along the way. 'Kill me, Rudy,' she moans. She repeats this plea several times, with much emotion and sincerity. I should like then to end with a slow fade to black.

"I look forward to hearing from you as soon as possible regarding the extra costs involved, and it is with great eagerness and anticipation that I await the finished product."

The letter closed with Rudy's best wishes and the loveliest of signatures.

Louie closed the folder and tossed it on the desk. Goldstick was beaming.

"You're a sick fuck," Louie said, with the makings of a grin at the corners of his mouth.

"Not me," said Goldstick, then he pointed to the folder: "Them."

"And in whose hip pocket might the international corporate headquarters of Dreams, Inc., be found?"

Goldstick, beaming wider, slapped his hip loudly several times in response. "If I ever do get even, Louie, *really* even, it will be through this. I am forty fucking years old next month." The beaming ended. "I have been busting my God-given balls in this shit-hole, making money for those greaseballs down the street, for longer than I care to admit." He gestured to the folder on the desk. "This is my ticket out of here. All those orders, all those checks, are from one single little ad that was published less than two weeks ago in *Penthouse.*

"See, getting laid is a thing of the past. People are worryin' about AIDS. I can't blame them. I mean, to die from drugs, from drink, that's stupid enough. But to die for a piece of ass? And these yuppies, the ones with the money, they don't fuck, except maybe once to breed when they reach the age of thirty-two-point-nine.

"What I'm saying is—and I've been in this racket long enough to know whereof I speak—your class person no longer fucks. Dreams, Inc., caters to that elite and affluent clientele. For a mere five hundred plus extras, Dreams, Inc., offers to fulfill any asshole's darkest, wildest fantasy. We offer him his dream come true, on a professionally produced, thirty-minute videocassette, which he can enjoy and cherish for the rest of his days until he drowns in his own spratz. Amen."

"And who's gonna make these tapes?"

"I already got him lined up, kid named Artie. He works for a guy out near me who does a lot of weddings and bar mitzvahs. He's lookin' to get started on his own. He's got all his own paraphernalia and he'll work for dirt. I'm settin' him up in a basement storage room down on Allen Street. The rent's nothin', two and a half bills a month. And the broads'll be next to nothin', too. Whores are starvin' these days, on account of the yuppies and the AIDS, like I say. I'm tellin' you, Lou, this could be it for me. Some more ads, an okay from Visa and MasterCard, I can be takin' in two, maybe three grand a week — for starters."

Louie looked at him. His uncle's words about the business of dreams moved through his mind like a shadow.

"Well," he said, standing, "you'll have cut rates for friends, I hope."

"Sure." Goldstick snickered in a cockeyed way. "You got a fantasy?"

"Yeah," Louie said. "Ten guys. I don't care what they're wearin'. They all pay me what they owe me."

The morning had turned into a day that was blue and clear and breezy. Louie walked downtown to the bar where those who sought him knew to find him. It was an old, out-of-the-way place called Mona's, owned by a Brooklyn man known as Mr. Joe, a cousin of Il Capraio's, who crossed the river only rarely.

The daytime bartender, a middle-aged man reputed to have been a master forger, spoke even less than Louie and, while otherwise highly professional in his service, he was adamant in his reluctance to foster business or wheedle tips by stooping to engage in the amenities of casual intercourse or illusory bonhomie, all of which he dismissed generally as "pulling these monkeys' pricks to shake a dime out of their assholes." This attitude, which would have made it impossible for him to tend bar most anywhere else, seemed not to bother Mr. Joe.

He brought Louie a glass of club soda with a piece of lemon in it and put two envelopes before him, each bearing the name of the man who had left it. Louie looked at the names, then removed the money, counted it, and stuck it in his left pocket.

A garbageman entered in a green garbageman suit with an orange garbageman stripe across his back.

"Put out your can, here comes the garbageman," Louie intoned.

"It's sanitation. *Sanitation.* How many times I gotta tell you? I'm a sanitation man."

The garbageman took out money and counted it while the bartender put a V.O. on the rocks in front of him.

"Garbage is garbage," Louie said. He reached out and took the garbageman's money; then he counted it and put it away.

The garbageman finished his drink and gathered his change slowly, hoping that Louie might buy him a shot. Leaving two quarters on the bar, he stood there, lingering, still hoping. Louie looked at him. "What are you waiting for? A receipt?"

"Just thinkin'," the garbageman muttered, then walked out.

"I hate garbagemen," Louie said.

"The only thing cheaper than a fuckin' garbageman is a fuckin' cab driver," the bartender said.

That was their conversation for the day.

A short black man wearing a hat made out of a paper bag ambled in and patted Louie on the back.

"Here's my friend." He grinned.

The bartender held up a bottle of Myer's Rum, and the black man nodded eagerly.

"Got a hundred for me, Lou?"

"For you, Pete? Anything."

The black man nodded happily and drank his drink. As Louie counted out five twenties, he looked into the mirror and adjusted his paper hat.

"How you want to pay this time?" Louie held the money just beyond the black man's reach.

"Pay? I don't want to pay. I always light a candle and pray you'll get run over and die. It's a long shot, but, then again, a candle's only a dime."

"That's nice to know, Pete. But, just in case you get a dud candle or some shit, how do you want to pay?"

"Let's see. How about two weeks? What's that come out to?"

"Two weeks, twenty percent. Sixty dollars a week."

"How about three weeks?"

"Three weeks, twenty-five percent. Forty-two dollars a week."

"How about a month?"

The bartender, looking away, raised his eyes to heaven.

"A month, thirty percent. Thirty-two dollars and fifty cents a week. I'll give you a break, you can forget about the fifty cents."

"That sounds good. I'll take the month."

"That's what you always say."

"Yeah, but I like to hear them numbers."

Louie gave him the hundred dollars, and he began to spend it immediately, joining customers at the other end of the bar, buying them drinks, and feeding dollars into the jukebox. When the single-action runner came in, he gave him five dollars on the two, five on the two-one bleeder. Then he bought more drinks for those around him. He was their favorite Negro.

The man whom Louie next received had been his first customer, years ago. Known as George the Polack—so much of dignity, and no more, had he wrestled from life— he was a fat, woebegone longshoreman who was well past the age of retirement but who traveled by bus to Port Newark for work whenever there was work to be had. He had borrowed against his pension to pay off his gambling debts but had gambled away that money, too. He would die a debtor. He knew that. And, until then, he would eat cheap meat and drink cheap beer, and even go without, just to pay the vig of his doom. His sad and bleary sunken eyes seemed to see nothing but that doom. He was cursed that way—born a fool, but not fool enough to hope.

"They garnisheed my pay," he said.

Louie looked at him, at those eyes of martyrdom in that big, drooping ham-colored face.

"The union rep said it wouldn't happen, but it did."

"Sit down, George."

George sat down.

"You're a nice guy, George, but you're a fuckin' idiot. You're an old fuckin' idiot, and if you had any brains, you'd blow 'em out. That would be the best thing, George. I mean that sincerely, as a friend."

Louie enjoyed this. George did not.

"Three weeks ago, you said you wanted five hundred dollars. I asked you if you wanted it on points. That way you could take forever to pay. No, you said, you'd pay me in five weeklies, thirty percent straight, a hundred and thirty a week. That's what you wanted, right, George?"

George nodded disgustedly.

"So, that's what you got. And what happens? Last week, you give me a hundred, you're thirty dollars short. What was it again?"

"The vet."

"Right, the vet. I sympathized with you, George, right? I

understood. A guy like you—old, alone, no friends, so ugly he probably never even got to eat pussy without payin'—a guy like that, he needs a dog, I told myself. A guy like that, his dog gets sick, it's a big deal. You see, George, I care. All my life, that's been my ruin. People walk on me, people take advantage of me—people like you, people who walk around bent over picking up dogshit, people nobody cares about but me. If it wasn't for me, your dog could be dead right now. Then where would you be? You're already a man without love, a man without reason to live. You'd be a man without dogshit, too. A decent person, a human being, would show up today with a hundred and eighty, maybe two hundred—the hundred-thirty for this week, the thirty from last week, plus a few pounds extra—'Here,' a decent person would say, 'buy yourself a little dog of your own. I appreciate what you did for'—what's that mutt's name?"

"Cynthia," the Polack mumbled.

" 'I appreciate what you did for Cynthia.' That's what I was hoping to hear. Instead, I get fucked."

"Nobody's fuckin' you."

"No, huh?" Louie's voice was different then. There was neither humor nor cruelty in it. "You're an old pro at this, George. You been in the hole, borrowin' and dodgin' since before I was born. You know the routine, and I know you. So let's cut the shit. When are you gonna make good?"

"Next week," George said wearily. In the sound of his words, there was as much loathing for himself as for Louie. "If the union don't help me, I'll figure out somethin' else."

The door opened, and in came two tiny men of obscure ethnic origin. One wore a double-knit suit the color of pale tubercular phlegm. The other, the younger and jauntier of the two, wore stiff, oversized designer jeans, turned up a good four inches at the cuffs, and a black T-shirt emblazoned with the words SEX MACHINE in bold shocking pink.

Each of the little men gave Louie a ten-dollar bill. He winked at them, in the American way, bringing expressions of giddy purblind deference to their faces.

"Decent people," Louie told the Polack as they swaggered out in miniature.

As the afternoon wore on, Louie entered into two new loans: one for two hundred at thirty percent, to be paid off in a month at sixty-five dollars a week; the other for a thousand at ten points a week, every week, for as long as it would take the borrower to repay the thousand in one single, full payment. Louie knew that both men were good payers, in different senses of the term. He knew that the one would pay on schedule, and that the other would take at least two months to pay, thus assuring Louie of a minimum return of eighty percent on the principal.

It was a good day for Louie. But when the spring light began to dwindle with the paling of the sun, the world through dirty windows seemed to darken and assume the colors of some awful thing just beyond remembrance, something that brought with it a chill. It came slowly then to his mind, the picture of foreboding and gloom at the foot of his uncle's stairs; and then the breeze at his neck seemed to be the very breath of that gloom and that foreboding. It rose, it fell. Then suddenly it swelled, gusted from behind black curtains by a brooding that was darker still. He inhaled that breath and that brooding, as if to seek in their mingled scents the trace of a more elusive scent, the scent of his own errant fate. But, in the end, it all smelled alike: spilled booze and smoke.

When the telephone rang, Joe Brusher had his hand on his cock and his eyes on the ass of a woman in a Diet Coke commercial.

It was Il Capraio.

"You're gonna have to go out there, Joe. You're gonna have to give him a good sittin'-down and find out what the fuck is goin' on."

Joe Brusher's face slowly budged with the faintest of smiles.

"Saturday," he said. "I gotta go out there anyway."

He turned around. The woman's ass was gone.

Donna didn't want to eat the Chinese food Louie had bought. She didn't want to watch the news. She didn't want to fuck and she didn't want to suck. She wanted to do what Louie dreaded. She wanted to talk.

"You know, Louie," she said, in that tone of voice that Louie was convinced had come from seeing too many movies and talking to too many vegetarians, "after all this time, sometimes I feel like I really don't know you at all."

Which movie was that one from? He stuck his fork into a carton of what was either General Tseng's Chicken or Triple Pork Delight. He brought it to his mouth; it was chicken.

"What size shoes do I wear?" he asked.

"Nine and a half wide," she answered.

"Well, see," he said, "that's something I don't even know myself. I can never remember it. I can only remember the wide part. Whenever I go buy a pair of shoes, I have to get measured. What I'm saying is, when it comes right down to it, you probably know a lot more about me than I do."

"Goddamn it, I'm not talking about shoes," her voice snapped and rose. "I'm talking about life."

"Oh," he said, not quite nastily enough to provoke further vexation. And as he chewed, he thought: Together again for one fucking week, and back to the same old shit.

"We fight, we fuck, we laugh, we eat, we sleep," she droned.

"Well, that seems to cover just about all our options," he said matter-of-factly.

"But where are we going, what're we doing? Where does it all leave me? You go off by yourself and you hang around with your sleazy low-life friends—"

He shot her a look.

"Excuse me, Louis," she said, testily indulging him. "Your sleazy low-life acquaintances." She breathed through her nose. "You go off and you do your little deals, and you disappear on your little benders, and you come back with that smile of yours and I melt in your fucking arms and I make believe that everything is rosy, and in the meantime, my life is going down the drain."

General Tseng's Chicken and the Triple Pork Delight were fast losing their flavor, which had been less than irresistible to begin with; and Louie put down his fork. He took a long swig of beer and leaned back.

"The first time I ever laid eyes on you, Louie, I felt fire." Donna was leaning back too now, and her voice was more relaxed. "Fire. That's the only way I can describe it. And you made me happier than I'd ever been before. But you also made me sadder, Louie, and you made me crazy. You brought me to the verge of a dream come true, then you drew back the curtains, and there was a stone wall two feet thick. You know what it's like trying to love a stone wall, not knowing what's really on the other side, or if you could ever even break through it?"

She looked at him. There were tears in her eyes. He took her in his arms and stroked her head, feeling her body jerk as she cried. He kissed her forehead, then the tears on her cheeks, and she began to laugh a little, in a melancholy way.

"What's that Italian word for *shylock* you told me?" she said. Her voice was soft.

"Usuraio," he said, letting the diphthong and final vowel roll slowly and luxuriantly.

"It makes it sound so pretty."

"Donna," he sighed, with resignation and impatience in his voice, "this is not what I plan to do for the rest of my life."

"And what is it that you do plan on doing, Louie?"

Her blond head turned in the crook of his arm, and she watched him peer out the window into the nighttime sky. His eyes seemed to grow cold, as if in dark concordance with something wicked in that sky; and she slowly drew away.

"I don't know," he said. There was an eerie, battened calmness in his voice. "They got a lot of pretty words in Italian."

Her eyes narrowed with a coldness of their own.

"See, Donna, you've got a lot of ideas about what's right and what's wrong and what's good and what's bad in this world. They're very fashionable ideas. Don't get me wrong. I think that's nice. I really do. I like fashionable women. But there are things that are a lot older and go a lot deeper than fashion."

"What are you saying?"

"You use words like *sexism* and *racism*. Those are very fashionable words. But they're words that didn't exist in the days before television. They're jargon. And I just don't put much faith in people who see right and wrong in terms of jargon. You can't reduce this world to a bunch of cute little fuckin' *isms*. You're just here for a fuckin' second— twice around the fountain and into the dirt, that's it. Good and bad's been around for a long, long time. You got about as much a shot at even beginnin' to figure out good and bad as you got at givin' immaculate birth to the Pep Boys.

"Before there were gods, there were goddesses. Men have always cursed women, and women have always cursed men. Maybe it's because each has power over the other, and each feels the power of the other is stronger and hates them for it. Maybe it's because the one is just the lost part of the other, and they hate that loss, or maybe they just hate themselves and turn that hate on that other part of themselves, the man on the woman, the woman on the man. Who knows.

"And before there was Rome, there was Carthage. Black and white have always fought, and whenever the one has had the chance, the other's been reduced to slavery. Don't think that slavery's a thing of the past, either. Only the fashion's changed. A man who works his life away to put food on his table and a roof over his head is still a slave to his master, even if, every Friday for ten minutes, he gets to hold a few of the master's dollars before giving them back over for that food and that roof. Sure, if he's lucky, he can buy out. But that's an opportunity slaves have always had —they've always been allowed to buy their freedom with money.

"Hell, the cabins Thomas Jefferson's slaves lived in were bigger than my apartment. I read the dimensions once, and I measured.

"See, it's not so much black or white. It's slave and master. Slaves and masters have always been every color. It's like men and women maybe, black and white. Maybe that's the way they hate themselves. Because, see, masters don't hate slaves. They love slaves—or so they say. Of course, they don't use that word, *slave*. It's gone out of fashion, like *master*. But a rose is a rose is a rose.

"Look at the Kennedys, people like that. They tell us we're all equal. But you'll never see a shine in Hyannis Port, unless maybe he's wearin' white gloves and carryin' a silver tray. The dogs would tear him to pieces. Equal pieces, of course. See, what they mean is that we're all equal under them. They're the ones—them and the black Kennedys, the Jesse Jacksons—they're the ones who keep talkin' black and white. They can't let people see—maybe they can't see themselves—that it's black and white and them. It's their money everybody fondles for ten minutes on Friday night.

"Whatever the truth is, it's got nothin' to do with right or wrong or good or bad. It's just something that is, something that's just there, like blood in the vein. It's got nothin' to do with whether you like it or not. The basic truth is that you were born to die. Why should any other truth be any less awful? Whining about 'deathism' isn't gonna add a minute to anybody's life, and none of those other *isms* are gonna change a damn thing, either.

"You can't fuck with the way it is. You can't turn night to day with ideas or talk. You just can't do it, Donna.

"But you like your fashionable ideas, and you like to talk those words."

It came back to her, as she had known it would.

"You watch TV," he said. "You read books, you go to movies. That's where you get your ideas. Instead of buying your freedom, you pay money to sit in the dark and watch a bunch of fruits with capped teeth playact in a goddamn fairy tale, and you think it's real. You read a book by some fool who thinks he's got somethin' new to say three thousand years after Babel, and you go right along with him.

"You know how on the six o'clock news, they always got one Yoo-Hoo—colored shine, one standard regulation Jockey-brief—wearin' white man, and either a round-eyed Chink or a spic with a peach-fuzz mustache, and one of them's always a broad? Well, sometimes, Donna, you sound like the broad. Sometimes, Donna, you even look like her."

She inhaled coldly and smiled. It was a smile like a drawn sword. "You attack when you feel threatened. You know that, don't you, Louie? All I did was ask you a simple question. I didn't mean to scare you."

She turned the blade of her smile slightly, letting it gleam menacingly in his eye.

"I'm only trying to explain something, Donna."

"You could have fooled me. You sound like a fucking third-rate mouthpiece for the Albanian Flat Earth Society."

He sighed.

"So, go ahead," she said. "Explain. Tell me why you keep saying things are going to change but they never do. Just tell me that. I don't want to hear about Jefferson's slaves or the six o'clock news or why the Kennedys suck or why I suck. I just want an answer."

Her voice had risen, and he glanced at her ominously. Then, against her silence, he breathed with disgust.

"Look," he said. "It's like this. You believe in certain things and I believe in certain things. You're the product of your ideas—"

She drew a sudden, jagged breath, as if she were about to erupt.

"—and so am I."

Her breath relaxed.

"Whether those ideas are right or wrong, or whether they just seem right or wrong to us, is something we'll never know. There are ways ingrained in you, and there are ways ingrained in me. Sometimes—often—those ways coincide. Sometimes they don't."

He was thinking of the old ways, ways that had served and been served by Il Santo of the legends and Il Santo's kind and in a manner old Giovanni, too. A part of him, obdurate and proud, had always believed somehow in those old ways, had somehow always felt that his true will's wreaking might lie in them. But another part of him, he knew, wanted only deliverance, only the soft breast's solace within his reach.

"Old ways are good ways," he heard himself say.

"Louie, Louie, Louie," she groaned in dire trochees of anger and despair. "Those ways are ugly ways. Don't you see? They just breed more ugliness and evil."

He hated hearing his name uttered that way, like a curse, like an abomination unto God.

"They'll make you ugly and they'll make you evil."

That hated utterance echoed still.

Donna moved her hand slightly, softly toward him. But he suddenly stood, and her hand jerked backward, as if from fire, or from a snarling dog. Louie walked two paces, and he waved sidelong at her in surly dismissal.

"Your father should've shot his fuckin' load into the sink," he sneered.

"You dirty fucking bastard," she hissed.

"Shut the fuck up before I shut you up." He felt blood pounding in his neck and head. "You got nothin' to say worth hearin'. You never did. If I had half a fuckin' ball between my legs, I'd put a muzzle on you and take it off just to let you suck cock."

"I used to think of you as a person with an ugly animal inside you. Now I know. You're just a fucking ugly animal. If I didn't hate you, I'd pity you."

"Well, shit"—he looked at her with a smile fit to break the steel of her own with a single blow—"I guess that doesn't say much for the people that swallow my scum."

Then, down on the street, the noise could be heard through Donna Lou's open window. The growling and yelping and howling were such that a little boy who did not quite disbelieve in werewolves clutched his mother's hand.

The noise ceased, but the thunder in the air did not. So, this was it, finally and for good, they thought, she in her way, he in his. Louie stalked out. The door slammed shut behind him. Nearing the bottom of the stairs, he heard it creak open—softly, timorously even—and he turned, grinning inwardly, as if to savor her surrender. The green beer bottle smashed into the wall, missing him, but not by much.

Joe Brusher's maroon Buick gleamed in the Saturday noontide sun, sailing east from Newark on 1 & 9, over the bridges to Jersey City, toward New York.

He parked on Grove Street near Bleecker, and he walked around the corner to Gristede's supermarket. Striding to the meat cooler in the back of the store, he scanned the parcels of pink and red flesh on display. He lifted several of them for closer scrutiny. At last he held a small loin of pork in his hands. He loosened its Saran wrapping and he carefully trickled the leaking blood onto the cuff of his shirt. Then he left the store and walked east on Bleecker, then slowly south, to the black-curtained place of Il Capraio, letting the sun dry the bright blood along the way.

As Joe Brusher entered, Il Capraio was sitting with two squat men in identical brown fedoras. With his right hand, Il Capraio gestured for him to stay but to maintain his distance for a moment.

Amid a flood of hushed Sicilian, Joe Brusher heard the address 9 Pell Street, and soon he heard Il Capraio ending the conversation, telling the fedoras *"Niente da fare, è l'unico modo"*—there was nothing they could do, this was the only way. The fedoras shrugged and nodded to express begrudging acquiescence. They rose, shook hands with Il Capraio, then left. Il Capraio waved disgustedly at their vanished backs.

Joe Brusher made himself a drink, letting Il Capraio notice the dried blood on his cuff.

"You ain't gonna believe it," he said after sitting down and taking a sip. "I mean, you were right, but you're still not gonna believe it."

Il Capraio looked at him inquisitively, narrowing his eyes, almost smiling.

"He made a deal," Joe Brusher said. "He went to bed with New York State. That drop in the numbers action out there? It ain't no drop, Frank. He's layin' off part of the action with the legal numbers here. He's got some of the shine bosses in cahoots with him. They're passin' the street-number action to New York State, through a couple of guys near the top up in Albany.

"The way they work it is if somebody bets a buck on seven-eleven, Brooklyn, through Giovanni and his friends, that becomes a dollar on seven-eleven in the legal New York State drawing. If seven-eleven turns out to be the Brooklyn number that night, they pay the guy off outa their pocket. If it don't come out, which it likely won't, they collect a commission from Albany, a dime on a dollar, just like they would if they'd put the bet in as a Brooklyn number with the boys. Meanwhile, if seven-eleven turns out to be the legal number that night, Giovanni and his friends hit and keep the money.

"Multiply this by a hundred thousand a day, a dime on a dollar, plus all those free State hits and the extra spread since the State's got no cut numbers. You got yourself a pretty nice racket. I figure that he himself's gotta be clearin' between five and ten grand a week."

Il Capraio's jaw dropped ever so slightly, and his face seemed to turn to stone.

"But that ain't the half of it, Frank." There was a wicked kindling in Joe Brusher's dark eyes, a kindling that transfixed Il Capraio's stony features all the more. "Get this:

He's gonna fix the legal number. Him and his lopsided friends in Albany, they figured out how to fuck the State."

Il Capraio looked straight into Joe Brusher's eyes. He thought of those three zeros on that December day long ago, and the nape of his neck turned to gooseflesh, as if that dark winter's wind had just blustered free from the grave of the years.

"You watch how they get that number when they show it on TV at night?" Joe Brusher was saying. "Them three gizmos with the Ping-Pong balls, and the broad calls out the number of the ball that gets sucked to the top of each gizmo when they turn on the juice?"

Il Capraio nodded slowly, still transfixed, still cold as stone.

"Yeah, well, there's ten of them Ping-Pong balls in each gizmo, numbered one to nothin', right? You take a hypodermic, shoot a few drops of hot wax into nine of them balls, and that leaves just one little old ball that's got a chance of risin' high enough to get sucked up into that bimbo's hand.

"You gotta admit, Frank, it's sweet."

"He told you all this, just like that?"

"He didn't say shit until I was halfway done smackin' him. Then he broke down. He told me he'd let me in on the fix if I dummied up to you. He wanted me to tell you that there's nothin' goin' on out in Newark, that the numbers are just dyin' out there and that's all."

"And what did you tell him?"

"I told him I'd think about it."

Il Capraio was silent then. Joe Brusher finished his drink and looked away indifferently.

"All right, Joe," Il Capraio said at last. "You tell him you thought about it. You tell him you thought about it and you want in. You find out what's involved and then you get back to me.

"You and me, we'll cash in with him. Then we'll cash him in."

"That's what I was hopin' to hear, Frank," said Joe Brusher sincerely. "That's what I was hopin' to hear."

Through the window, the twilight sky above Newark was shot through with a glowing violet wisp.

The shining black telephone on the table near that window rang, and old Giovanni, not moving his eyes from the eerie glow, raised the receiver to his ear.

"He bought it," he heard Joe Brusher say.

The Holy Week churchbells pealed in the campanile. Down the street, behind black curtains, Il Capraio oversaw his annual charity of the palms.

The dried fronds, still wanly green and supple, had been sent to him in tribute by another, mightier man who sat behind black curtains, on a street farther south. The origin of these palm leaves, which arrived in plenty each Lent at that mighty man's door, was said to be the pope's private stash in Rome. In reality, they came from a plant store on Sixth Avenue in the Twenties, whose owners, for two generations now, had lived in perennial, if not quite constant, debt to the card-dealing thralls of that mighty man.

Il Capraio had dispatched one of the neighborhood schoolboys—it was deemed an honor and a good omen for a mother's son to be so chosen—to deliver the fronds to the three old women on the Street of Silence whose job it was to weave them into artful sprays.

For days and nights, the old women's weaving had gone on, transforming the fronds into lovely, intricate, furling, sweet-smelling flourishes. Each woman worked in her own way, the way she had long ago learned across the sea.

Now, on this eve of Palm Sunday, the three women came forth, dressed and gauzed in black, bow-legged and shrunken and hunched as if in constant, fated obeisance, arms full of sprays and sprays and sprays of palm.

Il Capraio awaited them, sitting on a chrome-legged kitchen chair on the sidewalk near his door. One after the other, they leaned forward, already bent, to kiss his cheek. He took the palms from them, rewarding each with a jar of brandied cherries. "Those are the good kind," he told them.

Early the next morning, between the first and second Masses, the palms, for all to see, were taken by a lackey to the church. There in the sacristy, they were blessed by the priest who supervised the parish's gambling operations. Then they were returned to the black-curtained place, to be distributed by the local numbers runners in the days to come, holy reminders of the beneficence and godliness of Il Capraio.

As usual, Louie took two of the palms that were consigned to Giacomo's joint. At home, he threw away the old palm that had gathered a year's dust above his bed, and he put one of the new palms, the more attractive of the two, in its place. On Good Friday, he took the other, along with the butchered lamb, to Newark. The old man smiled dimly as Louie laid the heavy brown paper sack on the table and with a grunt lifted the baby lamb from it in its bloody plastic bag. Looking into its dead eyes and battered face, he smacked his lips. Then he patted it, where the skinned flesh of its buttocks pressed against the plastic.

"I'll have Ernie's wife salt it tomorrow," he said as Louie stashed it in the refrigerator.

"Farouk speaks," Louie muttered with his back to him, knowing he could not hear him. The lamb this year had cost him more than the fifty dollars the old man had offered to give him. He had thought of this, riding west beneath the riverbed; and he had thought of other things as well.

Easter passed and springtime ended, and the breezes blew warm when nighttime fell.

Goldstick wiped the sweat from his brow, made an apologetic gesture to Louie, and continued talking into the telephone.

Louie wiped the sweat from his own brow; then he took a pile of letters from Goldstick's desk and he looked distractedly through them.

"Dear Sir, Ms, Mrs," one of them began. "I have all kinds of fantasies when I masterbate. One favorite is to have a woman masterbate while taking deep drags on a cigarette or cigar. Somemore is going into a Lutheran Church and having my woman naked except for a wrap around dress or short skirt and having her open it up or raise it where she is completely nude and then having her masterbate either in front of or on the alter. Then I would eat her all over and she would suck my cock and at the same time be saying *fuck you God* and send us to hell you *sonofabitch*.

"I have done this myself many times and enjoy it very much except for the sucking. I would truly love to meet such a woman and would love her beyond her wildest dreams. If you can find her I would like a movie of her as you advertize. If you can bring her down here I will be in the movie too. Otherwise use a actor. The Ronald Coleman type is my sort."

Louie shook his head and tossed the letters back onto Goldstick's desk.

"Look," Goldstick was saying into the phone, "I'm talkin' apples and you're talkin' oranges and we're gettin' nowhere. Fuck all this depreciation shit and just concentrate on the fucking cash, all right? Yeah, I know you know. Only sometimes you don't sound like you know." He nodded, stammering. "Good. Right. Look, I gotta go. I have somebody here. Right. You do that. Yeah. Terrific."

He slammed down the receiver and swore, then wiped his hand across his face, as if to erase all thought. He looked into Louie's eyes and he spoke with all the repose that he could muster. "Louie," he said, "have you ever known me to stiff you?"

"No," Louie said. "I have never known you to stiff me. Your rating is good. But the day grows old, son of David, and you are about to work up to a touch in the inimitable, winding way that is yours alone; and I don't have the time for a play-by-play account of last night's Yankees game or a gate-to-wire rerun of yesterday's late double at Belmont. So cut the shit and spit it out. How much?"

"Seven grand," Goldstick blurted.

Louie did not blink, but he felt his stomach twitch suddenly. It was true that Goldstick was a good risk, and it was gratifying to find that Goldstick thought Louie did business on such a scale. But, at the same time, a loan of this size would leave Louie cash-dead if it went bad. He rubbed one eye and gestured with his chin toward the small stack of letters on the desk.

"How's this shit goin'?" he asked.

"It's goin' good," Goldstick said. "It's goin' real good. But I ain't."

Louie inhaled and he slowly nodded, multiplying and dividing in his head.

"Seven straight across," he said finally. "Seven points for seven weeks, then the seven grand in full."

"Seven!" Goldstick exclaimed, as Louie knew he would. "Five for five. I can pay you back in five."

"Six for five. And that's it. If you don't want it, go see Phil Rizzuto."

Five weekly six-point payments of $420 would bring a profit of $2,100, or thirty percent, on the seven grand in little more than a month. It was as sweet a deal as Louie ever had cut.

Goldstick snorted sardonically, looking at the image of his dumpy wife and progeny, loathing himself. Then his expression went blank and he nodded his assent.

He was still wearing that same blank mask on the night of the following day, when he came downtown to pick up the money: a pack of fresh hundreds, a quarter of an inch thick, which Louie handed to him in a manila payroll envelope from Chase Manhattan Bank.

There was something about that pasty mask that Louie did not like. At first, it reminded him of a mask he had seen before, on a man who soon after was found dead, self-killed. The troubling thought occurred to Louie that Goldstick might end up taking the seven grand with him to the big side bet in the sky. But when Goldstick, still wearing that mask, showed up a week later with the first $420 payment, Louie's fears were allayed. Goldstick, he then told himself, was truly a sucker of the finest moral fiber; he had been wrong to doubt him, even for a moment.

It was not until the third week—it was the dead of August—that his fears were dredged again to the surface and suddenly confirmed.

"I don't know how to tell you this, Louie," Goldstick said on that dank and dismal day, striving vainly through his mask to make light of what was incontrovertibly dark, "but there's another shylock in my life."

That vain attempt withered before Louie's silent glare, and Goldstick swallowed hard.

"I'm in over my head," he said. "The Stanley Cup play-offs killed me this year. I plunged, and I got cleaned out. Bonds, IRA, *il materasso*, everything—it all went to the fuckin' donkey. Meanwhile, I was five months in the hole with payments and penalties on my mortgage loan. The bank was threatening to foreclose. I went to the guys down the street, and, in a fit of brilliance, I arranged to have my house robbed. This would have brought me maybe ten grand from the insurance company plus half of whatever the guys got for my wife's furs and jewelry, TV sets, the silverware. I figured they'd beat me there, but the insurance money would more than make up for it. I set up a perfect time for them to break in, while the wife and kids were at my mother-in-law's and I was here. But I didn't know that the asshole eye doctor next door spent half his time lookin' across into my windows tryin' to cop a glimpse of my wife's titties. He called the cops. And the cops came. And those guys down the street here ended up shakin' me down for four grand, which I did not have, but which they arranged for me to get through their very own lending institution. This lending institution, Louie, is not like you. This lending institution does not smile, Louie, as you sometimes do. This lending institution is a psychopath who once did time for killing a woman by ripping her womb out with his bare hand.

"And so there I was, between foreclosure and this un-smiling golem, with my pockets turned out. That's when I came to you. I figured that with a little luck, with a few nice parlays, I'd be able to pay up on time. But those parlays didn't come; and I'm back in the hole to the bookie and the bank. And most of all, Louie, I'm in the hole to you."

Then Goldstick was silent, and he looked falteringly to Louie's angry eyes.

"You suck," Louie said, with the sum of his heart's sincerity.

Goldstick sighed forlornly, penitently, and he shut his eyes for a moment to Louie's glowering stare.

"So, what do we do?" he said. It was almost a whisper.

"What do *we* do?" Louie declaimed in slow stentorian blasts. "*I* don't do a fucking thing. I go downtown and see a guy, and I tell that guy that there's a Jew uptown who sucks, and I give that guy that Jew's name and address. And *he* does somethin'. And if you think some guy who goes around rippin' open cunts is bad news, you're gonna love *this* guy."

Goldstick breathed deeply. The air conditioner was on high, but there was sweat on his brow and there was sweat on his upper lip.

"It's not like I *meant* to stiff you, Louie."

"It's not what you mean to do in this world. It's what you do."

And, though his menacing glare was unwavering, Louie wondered as he spoke just what in this world he himself was going to do. He knew his threats were empty while he uttered them. It was not any affection, any concern for Goldstick that stood in the way of his going to that black-curtained place, for Goldstick had wronged him and Goldstick deserved to pay. But Louie knew that to go to that black-curtained place with any entreaty at all would ultimately render him beholden to that place, and to the one whose place it was.

"I can pay you in six months," Goldstick said. "I'll cut out gambling and piggy-bank it. Just give me a break on the vig."

"You'd cut out breathing first," Louie snapped back. "I said five weeks and I meant five weeks."

In his own concealed despondency, Louie almost blurted that he could not afford to give him a break on the vigorish, that the seven grand was nearly all the money he had in the world; but he caught himself in time.

The telephone rang on Goldstick's desk. Louie put out his hand and told him not to answer it.

"And so..." Goldstick said. He paused after those words

as if he did not know how to end them, as if he did not want to end them. "You feed me to the wolves."

Louie stood and raised his arm to aim a wrathful finger, and his mouth opened to declare that wrath, and his own furious exculpation, in words that were not set in his mind but which were about to burst forth all the same, rising in a visceral torrent of pure, unmitigated indignation. But then, as Goldstick flinched before him, the tension in his raised arm slackened, and his voice when he spoke was mean but composed.

"Is this Dreams shit set up legit?" He lowered his arm and jabbed with his finger at the letters on the desk.

Goldstick nodded, and he knew then what was coming, and he closed his eyes and nodded again.

"Well," Louie went on, his voice still mean, still composed. "I'll tell you what's gonna be." He sat down again and he lighted a cigarette and he blew a plume of bluish smoke toward the sweat on Goldstick's brow. "You meet me tonight at the Napoli Bar downtown. You bring your accountant, you bring your stock-certificate book and your little leatherette pouch with your bullshit corporate seal. And you bring a pen. Either that or you bring half of the eight thousand two hundred and eighty fucking dollars you owe me. One way or the other, you be there, at eight o'clock sharp. Otherwise..." And here Louie ended his words and just shook his head with an air of grim finality.

So it came to pass that, at about half past nine that sultry night, Louie left the Napoli Bar owning fifty percent of Dreams, Inc., and holding a promissory note in Goldstick's hand for the sum of eight thousand two hundred and eighty fucking dollars, upon the fulfillment of which Louie's fifty-percent interest in the corporation was to revert to Goldstick at a premium of three percent of the note's value, compounded monthly. Until that time, half of the corporation's net profits, reckoned weekly, would go to

Louie. Furthermore, the corporation agreed to hire, at a salary of one hundred and fifty dollars a week, for the duration of Louie's partnership, an employee of his choice. Already, as he began walking north, he could see in his mind the toothless, thankful, conniving grin of an old pal who was about to be offered the job of his life.

At the restaurant called Casa Bella, Joe Brusher and another man sat together at a secluded corner table beneath a painting, acrylic on velvet, of a tearful clown.

The man who sat across from Brusher was quite bald. What little hair he had was slicked back in gleaming black strands from a still well-defined widow's peak, giving his otherwise dreary, undistinguished face a certain devilish look. From a gold chain around his neck hung the likeness, also golden, of a clenched hand with pinky and forefinger extended downward in the sign of the horns. Three small diamonds studded this *mano cornuta*; and the sudden rainbow glistenings from those little prismatic stones caught Joe Brusher's eye.

"My wife," the man said, pointing to the jeweled and golden hand with his fork.

Joe Brusher nodded obliquely. "I used to have one of them," he said.

"You don't wear it?"

"No. A wife, I mean. I used to have a wife."

"Oh." The man dug his fork into the bowl of tripe that sat before him. "I didn't know that, Joe. All these years, I never knew that."

"Yeah, well. I don't talk about it much."

"What happened? If you don't mind my askin'."

"She died. Long time ago."

"Like I said, Joe, I didn't know."

"Don't get the wrong idea. There was no love lost between us there." He cut into his steak, then chewed. "How can you eat that shit?'"

"This? Tripe? You kiddin'? I love it."

"It's got no fuckin' taste."

"The sauce, Joe. It's the sauce."

Then there was nothing but the sounds of their eating.

"Speakin' of sauce," Joe Brusher said after a while, "those *ubriacon'* I told you about, the ones that got that load of plastic guns, I think their price is ready to come down. They can't move 'em for shit."

"Plastic guns. Who the fuck wants plastic guns?"

"Nobody. That's what these assholes found out. See, at first everybody thought these fuckin' things were gonna be a big deal. They said you could bring 'em through metal detectors, nothin' would happen. But that's bullshit, it turns out. The fuckin' thing's got somethin' like nineteen ounces of fuckin' steel in it. It's got as much metal in it as a fuckin' Bulldog. They said it was the biggest-deal gun in a hundred years, 'cause terrorists would be able to take 'em on planes and all this shit. They had it on the TV and everything. But it was all bullshit."

"Maybe they meant Polack terrorists."

"Yeah." Joe Brusher poured red wine into his glass, emptying the bottle. He signaled to the waiter for another. "Anyway," he said, returning raptorially to his steak and his sautéed escarole and his fried potatoes, "they got all these plastic guns, these assholes. They go for about four hundred overseas, where they make 'em. These guys'll take two-fifty, bulk. They're talkin' three, I heard the other day, but they'll come down. And I tell you the truth, it's not a bad nine-millimeter. And I know you like them."

The man screwed up his face and shook his head. "All

my life, I ain't touched nothin' but Smith & Wesson." He screwed up his face again, shook his head again. "Why fuck with success?"

"I just figured I'd let you know."

"I appreciate it."

The second bottle of Barolo Riserva arrived. The devilish man pointed his fork at it. "Tastes the same as the cheap shit to me," he said.

"Yeah, I know." Joe Brusher shrugged. "Some guy was tellin' me about it. I figured, try it, what the fuck."

"I mean, it's good, don't get me wrong."

"Just drink it."

The man buttered a crust of bread and wiped at his bowl with it.

"*Scopata*, eh?" Joe Brusher grinned.

"The best part." The devilish man winked, chewing and mopping more bread through the sauce.

"You ever use a knife?"

"You don't need a knife with this."

"No, I mean..."

"Oh. No. I have trouble slicin' a roast beef. Why? You?"

"Nah. I was talkin' to this kid, though, the other day. Works for the man out in Staten Island. He's one of them Beetle Bailey types, one of them military nuts. Wears the fatigues, the little army *capolichi*, all that shit. I think he's more bullshit than poetry when it comes right down to it. But anyway, this kid, he said the best way in the world to do a guy, the fastest and the quietest and the surest, was to get up behind him and stick him right here"—Joe Brusher tapped his crown lightly with his index finger—"right through the top of the skull, straight down, through the brain. He said the best thing to use was a British Commando dagger, some shit like that. I'm tellin' you, this kid had some line of shit. I just kept lookin' at him, and he just kept bullshittin' away. I don't know where that old bastard out there comes up with these fuckin' *guagliones*, I really don't."

"What're you crackin' up or somethin', Joe? Plastic guns, knives through the head." The devilish man snorted and shook his head, still chewing. "Maybe you need a rest."

"A rest," Joe Brusher snorted back. "I feel like I been sittin' around in a hirin' hall for the last year. My life's turnin' into a fuckin' rest."

"Nothin' shakin'?"

Joe Brusher grimaced and shook his head.

"You don't get around enough anymore, Joe, that's the problem. You stay down here with Frank there, and you don't get around. You should come uptown once in a while, say hello, shoot the shit. You're a big man, Joe, but nobody sees you."

"Frank's a good man," Joe Brusher said. "He's one of the smartest guys I know, and he's always been good to me."

"You're right there." The devilish man nodded slowly, reflectively. "Frank's a good guy. He's been my rabbi many a time, I'll say that much. But sometimes, you know, it's like the old-timers used to say: The graveyard's full of good guys."

"What're you gettin' at?"

"Nothin', I'm not gettin' at nothin'. It's like you with the plastic guns, the knives through the head. I'm just makin' conversation."

His bowl was clean, and he pushed it away. He patted his gut and winked across the table. "We're livin', pal," he said. Then he belched.

"Yeah." Joe Brusher winked back. "That we are."

They ordered coffee and cake. The devilish man suggested that they make the rounds and have a few laughs. Joe Brusher waved his hand.

"I'm gettin' too old for that shit," he said. "Maybe next time. I'm just gonna head back to Jersey and hit the sack."

"See, Joe," the devilish man said with a grin, "that's what I mean about you. You don't get around no more. Here we are with scratch in our pockets, and there's booze out there waitin' to be drunk and broads waitin' to get their yaps plugged and aces waitin' to be pulled, and you're ready for the sandman. I don't know, Joe. You don't watch out, you're gonna lay down before your time."

"Like I said. Maybe next time."

"Yeah. Maybe next time."

Outside, on Hester Street, they patted one another on the back, then parted. It was going on eleven thirty, and it was still hot. The leaves on the scraggy little sapling that languished in its rectangle of parched dirt near the curb where Joe Brusher's maroon Buick was parked did not stir at all; and there was no moon overhead to be seen, only the black sky through a stifling, sulfury haze.

Joe Brusher got in his car and he pulled away. But he did not head for Jersey. He turned at Sixth Avenue, and he drove north, moving slowly through the haze, and the white smoke that rose in billows from underground, and midnight's pastel death-twitch twinklings. He turned east on Twenty-third Street; then he turned again on Madison, which at this time of night was a dark and desolate valley that was soundless but for the rumbling of a distant bus ahead.

When he came to Thirty-ninth Street, he pulled over and he shut off his motor, and he gazed into the window of the Blarney Rock Tavern, and he waited. The lonely light from that window made the street seem even more deserted, even bleaker than it was. Through it, Joe could see the short, middle-aged Puerto Rican man in a dirty white T-shirt and apron, washing down the steam table; and the short Puerto Rican could see him.

After about fifteen minutes had passed, the barman—a young Irishman with a shock of red hair, white shirt with sleeves rolled to his elbows, and the loosened knot of a dark tie visible above the bib of his apron—came to the glass door and unlocked it, allowing the bar's last three customers to leave, booze-glad and loud. Then the barman turned and no longer could be seen. Joe Brusher shifted his gaze slightly to the right and kept his eyes trained on the short Puerto Rican.

Soon the Puerto Rican nodded and waved toward himself with a fast, beckoning hand. Joe Brusher removed a small Colt revolver form his glove compartment. The silencer on it was longer than its barrel. Drawing in his gut, he stuck the gun behind his belt, then grabbed his jacket from the backseat. As he stepped from the car, he could see the Puerto Rican unlocking the bar door.

Joe Brusher entered the bar, turning the key behind him. From beneath the steam-table counter, the short Puerto Rican wordlessly, nervously removed a long, heavy shotgun and placed it in Joe Brusher's hands. Together they walked to the rear of the barroom, to the alcove where the rest rooms were. Brusher held the shotgun low, its wooden stock nestled in the crook of his arm, his finger on the trigger.

The young barman came through the men's-room door rolling down his sleeves. In that instant, Joe Brusher suddenly raised the shotgun, and the barman's mouth fell open and he froze, looking from the barrel hole of the gun to the short Puerto Rican's evil-grinning face.

"Get your ass back in that fuckin' shit-house and get that fuckin' take back outa there," Brusher ordered.

The barman returned to the toilet. With a shaking hand he took a small key from his pocket and unlocked the paper-towel dispenser above the sink. Inside it, atop the stacked towels, there was a block of wood, on which there rested a pile of money, bound by wide rubber bands in two neat parcels.

The barman was still shaking when he placed those parcels in Joe Brusher's outstretched left hand.

"Now get downstairs and get the real money outa the fuckin' safe. All of it. You ain't gonna be cashin' no paychecks tomorrow, pal."

The barman glanced at the Puerto Rican, and a wave of disgust passed across the fear in his pale, freckled face.

"I said go!" Joe Brusher hollered, jerking the gun's long barrel in that frightened face.

The barman flinched and went. With another key from his pocket, he unlocked the basement door. Then his steps were heard descending the creaking wooden stairs. He was gone for three or four minutes.

He returned with a brick-sized bundle of bills in his hand. As the door swung shut behind him, he dropped it; for there, on the floor before him, lay the Puerto Rican. A thin, lacy trickle of bright red blood ran from a small black hole in his temple.

The barman did not wonder how such a big shotgun could make such a little hole, and he did not wonder why he had heard no gunfire. He did not wonder and he did not think at all. He just stood there and trembled.

"Pick it up," Joe Brusher said.

The barman retrieved the bundle and gave it to Joe Brusher.

"Now you know I ain't fuckin' around," Joe Brusher said, working the bundle into his inside jacket pocket, keeping the shotgun leveled with one arm and hand at the young man's chest. "How's your memory? When it comes to faces?"

"Bad. Real bad," he replied in a thick, faltering brogue.

"Yeah, well, you just get down in that cellar, Danny Boy, and you stay down there a good hour and you remember that."

The barman nodded, and Joe Brusher dispatched him with a quick wave of the shotgun barrel.

"Go on," Joe Brusher said, behind him at the top of the stairs, holding open the door with his foot.

When the barman took his first downward step, Joe Brusher shifted the shotgun from his right hand to his left, and he took out the Colt, which was now in his side pocket, and he fired once into the barman's spine and once into the shock of curly red hair, and he stood and watched as the barman's body tumbled and thudded down the stairs. Then he let the door close.

He walked behind the bar to the sink, and he put down the Colt on the drainboard to let it cool. With a bar-rag, he wiped the stocks and barrel of the unfired shotgun, then he left it, butt-down, in the sink. He stuck the Colt back under his belt; then he grabbed an unopened liter of Johnnie Walker Black Label from a shelf, and he strode to the front door, unlocked it, and stepped out, peering up and down the empty, silent avenue. Then he got in his maroon Buick and he drove away through the haze and the smoke and the twinklings.

The fix is set for the third Monday of next month, the twenty-first of September. The real fix, the malarkey fix, the whole shebang. We've got to have his fifty grand by that weekend."

"Don't worry," Joe Brusher said. "We'll have it. He's like a broad waitin' for the milkman with this fuckin' thing."

Old Giovanni nodded sternly.

"You know what he said? Get a load of this. I fed him the whole line of shit, piece by piece, just like you laid it out. Forty-five of his fifty goes for the juice upstate, I tell him; the other five's alive at legit State odds, five yards on a dollar, less five percent for shoe leather. 'Five percent for shoe leather!'—I thought he was gonna have a fuckin' stroke— 'That's a hundred and twenty-five thousand dollars!' 'Yeah,' I tell him, 'but it leaves two million three hundred and seventy-five fuckin' thousand for you. Besides,' I say, 'it ain't like sendin' a kid down the corner for the *News* and *Mirror*. There's a lot of hustlin' involved.' 'Bullshit!' he says. 'The shoe leather's supposed to come with the juice. That's the fuckin' trouble with dealin' with the State—they buck you to death from nine different angles. Everything's like fuckin' taxes with those cocksuckers. What're we gonna have to do next with this fuckin' thing, fill out fuckin' W-2 forms?' 'Well, look,' I tell him, 'just think of it as more juice. That's what it really is, anyway, when you get right down to it.

Like you say, it's part of the juice. Just think of it that way.' 'No,' he says, 'I think of it as fuckin' taxes. And I pay enough fuckin' taxes already as it is to those cocksuckers upstate. So I tell you what, Joe,' he says, 'we'll let that five percent come out of your cut.' Imagine that? I put up a stink to make it look good, but I didn't take it too far. While he was carryin' on, it hit me that him gettin' a bug up his ass was the best thing that could've happened. He's the kind of guy, he don't really believe in somethin' until he thinks there' a butt-fuckin' hidden away in it for him. He's gotta find that butt-fuckin' and short it out, even if it ain't there. Otherwise, he just don't feel right."

"You're gettin' pretty wise there in your old age, Joe. That's what that five-percent routine was all about. And you played it right, too. I got to hand it to you. You tucked him in good, Joe. You lullabied the shorts right off his ass."

Old Giovanni inhaled, slowly and deeply, watching the steam rise from the container of coffee that Brusher had set before him. The paper cup's familiar lying words—WE ARE HAPPY TO SERVE YOU—usually made him smile inwardly, recalling the gladiators' words he had learned long ago and never forgotten: *Nos morituri te salutamus*—We who are about to die salute you. But this morning he did not smile inwardly. He merely sat and remembered and watched the steam rise.

"We take that fifty grand, Joe, and we divvy it down the middle. Then we kick in another twenty-five grand each to what we have."

He lowered his spectacles and peered over them at his companion. "And remember, Joe," he said, "these figures can't be played with."

"I'm almost there. Don't worry. I'm almost there."

The old man eased his spectacles back into place.

"We take our two fifty-grand bundles, and we put them to bed."

He brought his heavy hands together in a sudden smacking clasp before him.

"The rest will be history."

He loosened his hands and rubbed at the pain that his careless gesture had caused in his rheumatic joints. Brusher watched the miserable wringing of those hands with the vague expressionless fascination of a king vulture. Giovanni sensed this, and his hands fell still.

"La vecchiaia è carogna," he declaimed drolly. "You know that saying, don't you, Joe?" He did not look to see Brusher's slow, detached nod of affirmation. "Old age is carrion," he said, turning the adage to English. He looked then to the younger man. "I used to get a kick out of all those old sayings," he remarked wistfully. "Then they started coming true."

"Ah," Brusher grunted in what he fancied to be an amiable, shoring way. "You'll outlive us all."

The old man shrugged, as if he sincerely did not care.

"Anyway," Brusher said, "I mean, before you talk yourself into the grave here, let's get back to them two fifty-grand wads humpin' away under the covers there."

"You know, Joe, maybe I should make you one of those hi-fi tapes of this. Then you could sashay around all day listening to it on one of those bebop boxes like the tootsies haul around."

"Yeah? With all due respect, John, it'd sound like a fuckin' broken record if you did—'And the rest is gonna be history. And the rest is gonna be history'—'cause that's all you keep sayin', John. I been hearin' a lot about history and a lot of big figures, but I ain't been hearin' a whole hell of a lot of anything else."

"What's more important to you, words in your ear or money in your hand?"

Joe Brusher mumbled and turned his palms upward as if to God.

"You want it spelled out for you, Joe? Is that what you want? Because if I spell it out for you, you better make sure you don't do any elbow-bending or sleep-talking between now and then."

"I just want to know."

The old man drank some coffee and then he spoke.

"That third Monday, while our friend is watching the clock and waiting for that TV patootie to let those Ping-Pong balls fly, somebody out at Aqueduct is going to flick a few switches, and that computer tote is going to spit out a track handle ending in three digits that will just happen to be the Brooklyn number that came to me in a dream the night before.

"Seventy-five percent of our money has wings," the old man went on. "That's the way it has to be."

"Seventy-five percent off the top, or off the payoff?" Joe Brusher asked, exhilarated and confused at once.

"There's no difference," Giovanni said. His tone was that of a teacher weary of children. "Seventy-five percent of the stake, seventy-five percent of the take—for us, no matter which end they take it from, it amounts to the same thing. Twenty-five percent of a dollar times five hundred is the same as five hundred less seventy-five percent. Of course, to them, there's a difference. A big difference. Seventy-five percent of five hundred is a hell of a lot more than seventy-five percent of a dollar."

"That's what I meant," Joe Brusher lied. "That's what I was wonderin' about."

"Well, see, Joe, the way I look at these things, the less you wonder, the better off you are. But, between you and me, for what it's worth, I figure these guys are too savvy to try to take that seventy-five they get from us and throw it into the same fix. It would be too much. It would be too risky. At the same time, I'd be surprised if they didn't make out with the seventy-five grand we fork over at least as well, dollar for dollar, as we make out. I'd be surprised if they didn't make out better. There are a lot of crapshoots out there that pay off at a lot more kosher odds than the Brooklyn number. And they can be fixed, too, by guys who know what they're doing.

"Me, I don't know any of that fancy Wall Street shit, any of that cocaine shit. All I know is this. And I know that seventy-five grand is a lot of juice to pay when it's my own damn swindle to begin with. But I also know that it's been close to sixty years since the last time I pulled off a swindle like this. I was a kid then. I was strong and I was fast and I could get around. Now, *sono carogna*. I'm old and I'm slow and I can't get around. So I have to pay others to do what I can no longer do. To tell the truth, Joe, that's one of the reasons I brought you in on this with me, to have you take my back. This is it for me, Joe. After this, I'm throwing out the deck.

"So, anyway, like I say, let's just worry about us."

"One thing, though. This rigged number. When do you tell me what it is?"

"That afternoon, when the deal goes down. That's how it has to be, Joe. You understand. It'll be a number from the news, from the TV or the papers. I can tell you that much right now. A hot batting average, the death toll of a plane crash, some shit like that. Those are the kind of numbers that get the heaviest waves of action. It'll make our payoffs look a lot less suspicious. Also, the following day, Tuesday, is an off-track day in New York. Aqueduct'll be closed, and that'll buy us some more time as far as any suspicions there go."

"I thought maybe you'd have 'em rig three nothin's again, like that time they all talk about."

"Nah." The old man shook his head. "That number holds more bad memories for me than good. Besides, it's a cut number at half the banks our bets'll be going in through.

"Our number goes from here"—he tapped lightly at his temple—"to my man that morning. From my man, it goes to the punks who'll do the running around putting it in for us, a few dollars here, a few dollars there, scattering it through New York and Jersey, clear down to Philly; and it goes to our key man at the track. Those punks who do the scattering won't even see the big picture until it's gone down. And the guy at the track, our key man, he got his job at the N.Y.R.A. through Cuomo. He's got a lot on the line, and he isn't about to make any false moves." The sober look on the old man's face eased into a wry grin. "He's the kind of guy my friend and I trust most—a guy with his cock on a butcher block and us holding the cleaver."

"And you ain't tellin' me who this friend is, right?"

"For now, Joe, all I can tell you is I've known him a long, long time. He's way up there, Joe; and he's worth whatever share of that seventy-five-grand nut he swallows. He's good as gold, Joe. You know I don't say that about many."

The old man took a final sip of coffee, which was now too cool for his liking.

"So," he said with a long breath. "We got twenty-five grand on the rigged number. At five hundred on the dollar, less fifteen percent off the top for the collectors, ten of which goes as the usual tips to the runners, our take on paper is ten million, six hundred and twenty-five grand. Just over twenty percent of that—two and a quarter million—is guaranteed to us, in cash, that same Monday night. Anything after that, we'll be long gone: my nephew will collect."

"Where exactly do we get paid that two and a quarter?"

"We'll know that afternoon. I'll make sure it's on our side of the river."

Joe Brusher leaned back, as if satisfied with all that had been said. Then the first question, the most important question, he had meant to ask, came back to him.

"What's the split?"

"A million and a quarter for me, a million for you."

A million for you. Joe Brusher had never heard those words addressed to him before. In a lifetime of unequal splits, inequality had never sounded so sweet.

"And we're not sticking around for the balance of the payoff. I'm not anyway. If you want to, that's all right. I'll send flowers if the shit hits the fan."

"No." Joe Brusher shook his head. "I'm with you."

"One thing I'll need to know, Joe—for the tickets. Does your passport have your real name on it?"

"Yeah. Brescia."

Both men fell silent again. Then an unclean grin crept across Joe Brusher's face.

"When we vamoose, where does that leave your good-as-gold friend?" he asked through that snaky grin.

The old man breathed heavily, then deliberately and firmly answered. "It leaves him either a whole hell of a lot richer or it leaves him fucked. The way I look at it, that's as fair a damn coin-toss as any in life."

Joe Brusher's face slackened, and the unclean grin was gone.

"So," he said, "even if they don't make us, even if the other payoffs come, you figure good-as-gold won't fork our money over to your nephew for us?"

"Some of it. A good deal of it. But without us, he'd just tighten himself up more and more as the money came in. He'd be a fool not to. After that first payoff, it all turns into a long shot, anyway." Old Giovanni's voice changed then. It became less hard, less resolute, as he went on. "That's the only thing that leaves a bad taste in my mouth," he seemed to brood aloud. "Leaving my nephew to hold the bag, I mean. If and when they do figure out that this whole thing wasn't just dreambooks and two-dollar bets; if and when they do come looking for us and they come up empty;

if and when the shit hits the fan, that kid's blood could end up in his shoes."

"We coulda brought him in with us," Brusher said with a shrug.

"Ah," the old man said, shaking his head. "The kid's a busted valise. He's lucky he's got a pot to piss in. If he does manage to collect for us, he'll be like a pig in shit if we throw him twenty grand."

"Well, then, with all due respect, John, I guess it's like you say: a toss of the coin."

The old man said nothing. He was through, for now, with words.

Louie opened his door and shook his head softly and just as softly laughed through his nose.

"I still can't get used to you with those front teeth out."

"Come on, don't start. I feel funny-lookin' enough as it is. I'm startin' to get a fuckin' complex or some shit."

Louie saw that Willie was carrying some sort of a metal box.

"The other night," Willie said, "I went into one of them jerk-off margarita joints on Seventh Avenue, that Cucaracha Cab Company or whatever the fuck it is. I figured I'd have a few. So, there's this broad there, and I'm givin' her the fuckin' eye, and she's givin' me the eye, and all the usual shit leadin' up to the many-splendored thing. And then I smile and she almost chokes to death on a fuckin' ice cube. I'm tellin' you, if I ever run into that scumbag who hit me with that brick, I'm gonna feed his fuckin' balls to him, I swear to Christ."

"You were tryin' to rob the guy, what do you want?"

"Still, it ain't right." Willie turned down his mouth and shook his head indignantly. He shifted the weight of the object under his arm, then raised one knee and began to scratch at his shin.

"Sit," Louie said, after beholding this ungainly sight for some moments.

Willie sat on the couch and adjusted his socks.

"So," Louie said, "how was your vacation? Did you do the whole twelve weeks?"

Willie nodded disgustedly, trying to smile. "It was all those ninety-day suspendeds since the time before that fucked me." Then he livened, and he actually did manage to smile. "It was Secaucus, not that fuckin' house of horrors on Pavonia Avenue. That's the main thing. Secaucus ain't bad." There was even a trace of wistfulness in his smile now, or so it seemed to Louie. "If you go to Mass, they give you free jelly doughnuts."

Louie tossed his chin inquiringly and pointed to the box that Willie was holding. Willie put it on the floor, and his eyes widened with self-satisfaction as he gazed at it.

It was a gray metal rectangle, about ten inches by five, with a three-pronged electrical cord. On it were the words HIGH-SPEED TACHISTOSCOPE. It had a red POWER button; three switches, marked ON, INITIATE, INTERNAL; and two black dials, indicating RANGE and TIME IN MILLISECONDS. Louie looked at it for a long time; then he looked at Willie and said, "What is it?"

Willie stretched out his hands toward it and wriggled his fingers with greedy delight. "I don't know," he said, "but I bet it's worth a lot. It's got a lotta little knobbies."

"Where'd you get it?"

"St. Vincent's."

Louie shook his head. "Nine guys wired to the wall on the sixth floor probably croaked when you unplugged the fuckin' thing."

"Nah. It wasn't even plugged in. It was just sittin' there whisperin', 'Take me, take me.' I figured you might know what it was. You got a lotta smart friends. Maybe one of them might know. I can't sell it till I know what it is—I could get beat."

"Well, I don't know what it is. And I told you a long time

ago, I don't want to have anything to do with this sort of shit."

Willie looked at him slyly. "How'd you make out with that booze I gave you before I went away?"

Louie sighed. "What do you care? You owed me a hundred. I took the booze instead. That's that."

"We're even, then?"

"You might say that. Then again, you might take into consideration all the drinks and all the meals and all the smokes and odd dollars you been soft-shoein' me for all these years. We've known each other since we were, what, thirteen? When we were thirteen and a half, I gave you that dime to bet at the feast, remember? Since then, we've never really been even, I don't think."

"I paid you back that dime, you fuck."

"Admit it, Willie, you're a fuckin' mooch. And now you're funny-lookin', too."

Louie, who had been trying to keep a straight face, broke into a grin, and Willie, who had been about to begin stammering with exasperation, started to laugh.

Then they just sat there, with an ashtray between them, looking down at the gray metal box.

"You still with what's-her-name?" Willie asked after a while.

"Ah," Louie mumbled, grimacing.

"She seemed nice."

Louie nodded grimly, then exhaled some words: "Too much shit involved."

"There always is. Unless maybe you wanna get one of those inflatable ones."

"It's a thought." Louie grinned. "They got the lifelike mouth, the *come-si-chiam'*, the hole in the back, if you go for the Greek." He lighted a cigarette, the last in the pack, and coughed. "How about you? Your dick been anywhere interesting lately?"

"Nah. All the old familiar faces. Tell you the truth, Lou, unless I got a few in me, I really don't got much interest these days. I feel, I don't know, fucked-out or somethin'. This time last year, when I was drivin' the cab, forget about it. I don't think I ever got laid so much in my life. I don't know what it was. It was like there was a milkman strike or somethin'. Maybe that's what happened to me. Maybe I O.D.'d on pussy." His eyes drifted, and he began to giggle. "Did I tell you about the time I was drivin' the cab, I picked up the guy in the dress and let him blow me?"

Louie looked at him with one eyebrow raised. "You're fuckin' sick. You really are, you know that?"

"Hey, he had nice legs."

Louie snorted, smiling. He blew a ring of smoke toward the gray metal box. "I figured you would've had AIDS by now, between all those dirty needles you stick into yourself and all those mangy broads you fuck. Now that you don't even have your front teeth, I can imagine what the next love of your life's gonna look like."

"Fuck you," Willie laughed.

"What was the name of that one you brought around that time, the whore that shot the dope into the abscess on her gum?"

"Crazy Barbara. She thought junk cured everything."

"Right. Crazy Barbara. She's sittin' there, right where you are, complainin' that she was suckin' off some cop who popped her and he ended up pissin' in her mouth. Two minutes later, she offers me a swig of her beer."

"Yeah, she was a bit on the gamy side."

"You still foolin' around with her?"

"Nobody's foolin' around with her. She shot wine and died. Three weeks in a coma." Willie narrowed his eyes and nodded slowly. "You gotta admit, though, she had nice tits."

"That's as good an epitaph as any, I guess."

"You're more likely to wind up with AIDS than me. Half the broads around here where you live are fuckin' around with fags. I bet there ain't a woman in Manhattan under the age of forty who ain't been to bed with a faggot. I'm serious. Things are gettin' strange. We're an endangered species. We don't suck cock, we don't even jog. We're finished. Fifty years from now, they'll have a few of us stuffed up there in the museum behind plate glass, sittin' on a bench scratchin' our bellies and starin' at a pair of stuffed broad legs. There'll probably be a stuffed pigeon shittin' on our heads, to boot."

"You're a lot more talkative since you laid off the *bubbonia*, anybody tell you that?"

Willie smiled crookedly and tossed his head to the side.

"Maybe you should go into politics, run for assemblyman or some shit like that."

Willie laughed, low and unsmiling. "I better go into somethin'." He peered blankly toward the wall. "I used to think I was a good thief. I really did. Then one day it hit me: If I was such a good thief, I wouldn't be gettin' caught all the time. So, I asked myself: What am I good for? That's as far as I got, a question and no answer."

"Ah, we were both stupid," Louie said. There was a gravity in his voice now, a certain somber clarity. "We both thought we were smart. We thought fuckin' around was the main event. Now here we are. You, me, and the wall."

"And the box with the little knobbies. Don't forget the box with the little knobbies."

"Right. And the box with the little knobbies."

A siren wailed beneath the window on Bedford Street, then faded north. Louie and the other watched the faint spidery shadows of afternoon that were beginning to creep across the floor.

"Anyway," Willie said at last, "you said you wanted to talk to me about somethin'."

"I got a job for you," Louie said plainly.

"What do you mean, 'a job'?"

"A job. A fuckin' job. You heard the word before. It's how human beings usually make a living in this fuckin' world."

"Oh. A day job, you mean." Willie looked at him suspiciously. "Doin' what?"

"You're not going to believe this, but just listen."

Dreams, Inc., thrived. There seemed to be no end to the innumerable mutations of concupiscence that slithered forth like monstrous silverfish from the dank and odious broom closets of men's minds. Beneath Allen Street, in the seedy basement storage room that Goldstick, with three gallons of cheap white paint, a secondhand desk and chairs, and a telephone hookup, had converted into an equally seedy office and studio, palpable life—or something like it—was given to the inmost, profoundest sin-born imaginings of those sick fucks whose checks had cleared. At August's wicked end, after only two weeks of their bitterly begotten but sweet-flowering partnership, Goldstick and Louie, grateful to God and to the witless vileness of their fellow man, divided almost nine thousand dollars in profits between them. In hand were another thirty-four orders, worth seventeen grand, and the mailman brought more every day.

The presence of toothless Willie proved to be a boon of some worth. Though his blood remained clean—or so he claimed; Louie at times believed him, at times did not—Willie yet moved easily among the grim society of lowly junkies who haunted nearby Chrystie and Rivington streets. From that society of the undead, he already had managed to recruit three not unattractive girls who were more than willing to method-act in exchange for their poison's price—or for a thrice-cut parcel of the poison itself, as sly Willie occasionally arranged it.

"These girls are like dishrags! No resistance at all! It's great!" enthused Artie, the young wooer of the muses whose job it was to direct, shoot, and edit each videotape, and to fetch his superiors' lunch from Katz's Delicatessen. So pleased was Artie with the way things were working out, he did not even much complain the day one of his dishrags nodded out, stone-cold unconscious, while supposedly butt-plugging herself to ecstasy with a plaster statuette of the Blessed Virgin.

Louie was standing there that day, watching. It was the first Dreams, Inc., production—or "shoot," to use arty Artie's word—that Louie chanced to attend. Prior to the taping, the girl had oiled down the statuette with Crisco. The look of disembodiment in her lifeless eyes—methadone and wine and distant death's bleak lullaby—lent her slow, methodic lubrication an air of strange, grim ritual. Then, as Artie moved forward with his camera, the girl raised the Crisco-glistening icon to her open mouth and closed her lips around it, as she had been told to do. Louie watched, transfixed, as the girl drew the Virgin from her mouth and rubbed it across her scrawny breasts until they reddened. She moaned, as instructed, then brought the Virgin to her cunt, then to that nether hole. With two slow twists of her wrist, the girl put the walnut-sized head of the statuette into her ass. Little by little, as far as its prayer-clasped plaster hands, the Virgin's body followed. Slowly at first, then harder and more ferociously, the girl drove the gaudy statuette in and out of herself. The small praying hands stabbed into her perineum, again and again, until there was blood.

Louie looked at Willie, and Willie looked at Louie.

"Just think," Willie whispered to him out of the side of his mouth, "I'm bringin' it back to the *botanica* for a refund after this."

Then the girl's driving hand grew torpid, then fell still, and those listless, disembodied eyes were dead to the world. She lay there like a corpse, the Virgin sticking from her ass like a stake. For a moment, in fact, they thought she was dead. Methadone and alcohol, after all, was, as both Louie and Willie knew, a combination far deadlier than junk. And what a final pose this would have been.

Louie was not really needed in that basement, any more than Goldstick was. He knew that. The operation overall ran so smoothly, thanks to ill-paid Artie and worse-paid Willie, that Goldstick and he had little more to do at Dreams, Inc., than to pat those hirelings on the back and count money. And, to be sure, what Louie witnessed there on that day of the Virgin repulsed him.

But in that repulsion, there was an attraction too. More and more frequently, after his early morning coffee on the Street of Silence, he would amble east from Giacomo's joint to that pit of dirty dreams. He would sit and he would smoke, while before him among the makeshift props of the day, a girl—or two girls, or a girl and a boy—fulfilled some unseen and faceless masturbator's fantasy of lust. He would watch their eyes as much as the rest of them, and he could tell when a girl began to drift and swoon beneath the actual heat of illusion. It was then that he would feel an odd power, not only over the flesh that writhed in real or feigned prurience before him, but over, as well, those unseen, faceless fools whose pathetic passions were his to deride, whose money was his to hold; and it was then that his cock would stir.

But somehow this grotesque travesty of desire only deepened his sense of loss and the pangs of longing he felt for Donna Lou. Months had passed since he had heard her voice or touched her skin or seen her smile. That hearing and that touching and that seeing, it now seemed, had been all of beauty he knew in this world. It had been his.

"You look like Hamlet beholding Yorick's skull," Goldstick said to him late one afternoon as he sat gazing at the cover of a tawdry paperback that had been lying on the desk. The words startled him, and he tossed the book aside.

For as long as Louie had known Donna, she had returned in her reading to the same books—novels by Jane Austen and Henry James—again and again. Louie had come to know the covers of those Penguin paperbacks well. He had browsed the introductions to several of them, and one night had asked her with a cockeyed grin: "You only read books by people who never got laid?" Not long after that, Goldstick had been trying to unload a crate of old pulp smut at a quarter a shot. Louie, passing that heap of sleazy paperbacks, had stopped suddenly when his eyes chanced upon the cover of *I Married a Lesbian Slut*. Its author's name was Henry James. Goldstick had let him have it for nothing, and he had dropped it that night in Donna Lou's lap. "I bought you one you don't have by that guy you like," he had said with an almost convincing innocence. The book that had been lying on the desk this day, *Born to Hump*, also bore the name of Henry James. He had been staring at it, remembering how Donna Lou had laughed and softly shaken her head that night. Lost to the world, he had been trying to recall the sound of that laughter; but the sound never came.

Now here he was, fallen—forever, he felt—to this forlorn sideshow in a hole beneath the ground where some dim, fatal disease of the soul seemed to dampen the air like malarial miasma; where every voice lied and skin was ugly as snakes' in molt and every smile was false. More and more, the cold disfigurements of lust that slithered at his feet served only to remind him of what he had lost; and his cock, in time, no longer stirred with any sense of dwarf-king power. After all, he came to see, this was no kingdom, but only a makeshift hell of his own device. It would do for now, until the real thing came along.

Louie was sitting with his coffee at old Giacomo's joint at daybreak, adrift, when he realized that the old man had been talking to him without his hearing the meaning of his words. For days, the vein in his wrist had been beating hard. Or so it seemed. Maybe he had just been staring at it more than usual. He had been doing a lot of that lately—staring; staring, as if at blood on walls.

He had been shylocking now for nearly five years, and he had nothing to show for it. It was a rougher racket than he had ever dreamed it to be. After all was said and done, after the last column was tallied, after all the liars and stiffs and criers and *bustarelle* were taken into account, he probably would have done just as well sitting on a C.D. and scratching his ass for five years. But, to him, the easiest was always the hardest, and the hardest always looked easiest.

What, really, did he have to show for anything in this life? A few notches on his cock, some scars on his liver and his lungs? The way he figured it, by preternatural Albanian actuarial instinct, his life, at best, was half over. And the first half had been a bust. Reaping time was not that far away, and he had not sown. Past, present, future—a blur.

But in that blur—now bright, now dwindling, now

bright again—there was a spark that Louie always felt might rise to blaze, to consume that blur with a lovely burning all too clear. It was like an ember flickering endlessly between dying and kindling, burning to cool ash or to flame. Its smoldering ebbed but it never ended.

It had ebbed over the years with the burying, one after the other, of his blood; but, in time, when the grave-dirt hardened, it always glowed anew, and even a bit more strongly. It had ebbed not long ago, when, as the winds warmed, that gust had passed between him and what remained of his blood, that enigma behind the door atop those creaking stairs in Newark. But no gust, whether it was from some old man's soul or his own, or some cemetery hill, could kill it.

Donna Lou had been a bellows to that ember. Of course, he never told her so, for he sensed it would have given her power over him—or, rather, would have made her dangerously aware of the power that she already, unknowingly, held.

Maybe what he sensed was true, or maybe he was merely seeing through an evil eye. One thing was sure: He had all too often beheld Donna Lou herself through that eye. He had been prone to brood on and to inwardly catalogue her human imperfections: the birthmark behind her left knee; a liking for the moving pictures of the day; a tendency to bite her nails; a recurring credulity in what she read in the papers; the careless way she folded his laundry—in particular, his shorts; the eating of cottage cheese in his presence; and so on. This cataloguing of imperfections, he realized, served to enhance, or, more precisely, to distort his evil eye's vision. Somewhere, his evil eye had led him to think, there must be a perfect Donna Lou, a Donna Lou who folds shorts with the care and reverence of a sacristan folding altar linens on the eve of a holy day.

His evil eye saw only imperfection. His evil eye sought only complaint. It spied perfidy everywhere—thirty silver pieces in every gentle hand. By keeping him from trust, his evil eye, like all fine evil eyes, had protected him from falling prey to treachery. But it had kept him, too, from that inner providence, that human light called wisdom, without which mistrust was as ruinous as trust itself and as blind as trust could ever be. His evil eye, he had now begun to fear, had warded off what little good might come to him along with any evil, and it had nurtured inside him something worse than anything outside him to which he might fall prey.

In unspoken words and shifting, cursive shades of brooding, he had been pondering these notions more and more. It was—as now—not a deliberate pondering. It came and went; and when it came, it weakened his evil eye, and that ember seemed to burn. Slowly, he had begun to assay the weight of what lay beneath this pondering.

Just last night, lost in that brooding and that assaying, he had been sitting blankly before the TV. Suddenly, he caught a glimpse of Erin Gray, the lady in the Bloomingdale's commercials. To Louie, Erin Gray had always occupied a unique and exalted place—a throne, one might say—among the hierarchy of womankind. He had wanted to fuck her since that long-ago night when he had first seen her stroking that all-cotton sheet and purring about the white sale to end all white sales; had wanted to watch those bedroom eyes of hers flutter half closed beneath his own. Until the all-cotton sheets of earthly bliss bore the stain of their lust—or at least a quick blowjob—or until she started showing her age, whichever came first, his passion would not be allayed. But last night, glimpsing her as her luscious fingers graced an array of cashmere socks and her rosy-red lips parted moistly to tell of savings beyond belief, no glint came to his eye and he barely noticed when her thirty seconds were up. Desire, the lizard in his britches, had not even budged.

It may not have been the weightier, vaguer pondering alone that held him, for often this pondering was a vast and murky sea under a storm-colored sky of lesser but more lucid, more familiar concerns. The strongest color in that sky—more than a color: a rainbow-pinioned, upward surge of iridescent light that cleft the clouds—was greed.

Greed. There was no other word for it really, that golden stitching in fortune's skirt that all men coveted. Ambition, drive, the longing for success, or security, or advancement; the desire to do well, to make something of oneself, to provide for one's loved ones; even history's much-touted search for a short route to the Indies—these, Louie knew, were nothing but candied conceits that only the deluded or self-deluded could fail to recognize as sanctimonious euphemisms for greed. Men who denounced greed, men who saw their own avarice in terms of altruism were merely licking the wounds of their failure. Like ugly women who reacted to the blows of their own undesirability by decrying sex as pornography and by reviling their more fortunate sisters as victims, rather than as victors, of men; like failed artists who damned the taste of the masses and proclaimed their devotion to posterity; so these men, many of whom spent more on million-dollar-lottery tickets than on bread and wine for their tables, held themselves to be innocent of greed. "Money doesn't mean anything to me," these men would say, but they never had the scratch to prove those words. Usually, they were ten-percent tippers who worked overtime whenever they could and checked the floor for stray coins wherever they went. They were the biggest chiselers and the biggest stiffs and the biggest moochers in the world. Louie knew that, and he knew that greed was as natural, ineluctable a part of nature as lust. Like lust, it was as good or as bad as men made it. A man could rule it, or it could rule him.

It did not seem strange to Louie that the rainbow light of what he called greed should emerge from his vaster brooding. If improvidence and an evil eye were the interweaving curses of his life, perhaps these rays represented something of its hope. He knew what it said in Donna Lou's Bible, that "if thine eye be evil, thy whole body shall be full of darkness." And he knew what it also said, that "money answereth all things."

As much as he wanted money, and though recent weeks had brought him the biggest, most easily gotten pay of his life, he knew that his fortune did not lie in Dreams, Inc. It was, he knew, a fleeting thing, not meant to last. Nor did he really wish it to last. Sometimes, lately, bringing a piece of bread to his own mouth, his eyes would stop his hand, as if that hand were dirtying that bread.

No, his fortune, whatever it was, lay elsewhere, off in those rays, in that light. The trouble was, all light seemed lately to conspire to remind of the light, now gone, that shone in Donna's hair.

"It'll only be four days . . ."

For days on end? For days and days? Four days? Four days of light? Four days in hell?

"It'll only be four days," the old man was saying, looking straight ahead, expressionless, toward the wisps of early sun that crept beneath the lowered black shade of the door. "In Thursday night, out Monday mornin'. Just tests, or so they say."

Through the eddying haze of cigarette smoke that veiled the old man's profile, Louie saw him grimly smile, still peering straight ahead.

"They wanna look at this, look at that," the old man went on. "Take a piece here, piece there. They love them fuckin' biopsies, these characters. They don't do autopsies anymore. No money in 'em. But they sure love them biopsies. Open your fly to take a leak, they'll have a tube up your prick and a six-page bill pinned on your balls faster than a Chink can blink.

"Tests. Who the fuck are they kiddin'? The way I figure, at my age, they're just primpin' me for Perazzo. They wanna make sure they get a chance to shake me down good one last time, in case I croak nice and peaceful in my sleep without them havin' a chance to go through my pockets.

"Anyway, you know how it is with this kind of a joint. You shut down one night, you suffer for a month. People show up here at four in the mornin', come from God knows where to get here, some of 'em. They find a lock on the door, that's it. Fuck it, they figure. Next time, they hit a different joint. Especially a time like this, Labor Day weekend."

Louie apprehended now what the old man had been saying moments ago, while Louie was lost in his reverie. He had to go to St. Vincent's for a few days, he had been saying; and he had asked if Louie would fill in for him while he was gone. All the while, in his reverie, Louie had been nodding abstractedly in dumb response to the sound of the old man's voice. In doing so, he realized now, he had unknowingly assented to do what the old man asked. His immediate reaction to this realization was to recoil from the prospect of his commitment. Then, just as quickly, he relaxed. He had not worked for Giacomo now in over two years. In all that time, he had never regretted leaving. The money had been good, but the hours and the grief and the grind had been hell. Still, he occasionally missed the madness of working this joint; missed the wild nightly steering of this ship of lost souls down the old river Styx to dawn's cruel shore. Four nights of that—four nights only—might be fun; and the distraction might do him good.

"I'll give you two hundred for the four shifts, plus your cup. You know your way around this joint. I'll leave you stocked up. The bank'll be where it always was, in the box under the ice machine."

Louie listened as Giacomo told him whose checks had bounced lately, who had been eighty-sixed, who owed what, and who seemed to be headed around the bend.

"Same old shit," the old man concluded. "Nothin's changed since the last time you worked here. A few pretty ones got ugly, a few ugly ones died, and Budweiser went up a quarter."

Louie took Giacomo's spare key—the one key to the one padlock at the door—and he added it to the ring of keys he carried with him.

Running his thumb across the teeth of the key to the Allen Street basement, he began to walk north on the Street of Silence, planning to turn right at the next corner and amble east on the sunny side of the street to that hovel-hole of dreams. But after only a few paces, he stopped. He looked south over his shoulder. The immense gray tombstone towers of the World Trade Center rose in the distance.

A long time ago, when those towers were new, Louie had sold drugs down that way, catering to the young Wall Street workers who came at lunchtime to the yard of Trinity Church, where he and Willie awaited them near the big cross among the worn-away sandstone grave-steads. He was in love then with a girl named Mary who was a secretary at the French Line, not far from there. He used to sit on a bench in Battery Park on warm afternoons. He used to close his eyes and feel the sun on his skin and the breezes from the harbor where the rivers met. He had not been down there in years, but he remembered the bench where he sat, and he remembered how good the sun and the breezes felt.

He began walking toward those remembered things. He had all the time in the world, he told himself. After all, his life was only half over and he had already made it six blocks.

At this early hour, the storefront stalls of the Chinese grocers and fish-sellers that crowded the south side of Canal Street were already bustling. Louie loved the brash-mingling scents and colors of this dirty stretch of sidewalk stands; and it had been a long time since he last let himself enjoy them. There were boxes of black spiny urchins and mounds of sweet-smelling gingerroot, curly-leafed bundles of purple-veined kale and bunches of dried peppers the colors of fire, bushels of fat eels and baskets of small irides-cent quivering things.

He walked to Mott Street, then turned. He wanted to see if the Lime House, the last guinea joint in Chinatown, was still there. It was, looking much the same as Louie remem-bered it. He wondered if the fried squid and conch were still good and still cheap, if the hard-bread was still hard. Shading his eyes, he peered through the glass. The bar-stools were upended on the bar. A porter was mopping the floor.

How many sundowns had he sat at that bar, gorging himself and swilling, warming to the night's seduction, back when the night could still seduce? He could not count them, but he could recall those special dusks at this bar, when, through this window, the spell of the falling dark turned the Chinese neon outside to magic and whichever girl he was with was, for then and evermore, but mostly just for then, the goddess of his dreams. Then one night, that goddess next to him was Donna Lou, and nightfall's seduction was nothing to her own, and that Chinese neon seemed to be there just to cast its glow into her eyes.

He stood there a minute or so, watching the porter mop. Then he walked on, down narrowing Bayard Street to Baxter, then down Baxter to the old Five Points, through Foley Square, down Centre Street to Park Row, past City

Hall, to Broadway; straight down Broadway, past Trinity Church, past Bowling Green, to Battery Park.

At the Netherlands Memorial, he bore to the left. There, by a lamppost in that park's grassy northern end, was the bench he remembered. He slowed his pace as he approached it, smiling to see that it was vacant.

To the west was Pier A and its old red firehouse. But now, encroaching on the north of it, there was an unsightly, sprawling encampment of vans and junk heaps. The ground beneath them was part of the hundred-acre landfill, a ghastly man-made desert of debris, that had just gotten underway the last time Louie was here. Like the World Trade Center, whose excavations had formed the landfill's base, the towering tombstones rising here belittled what once had been big and further destroyed what character and majesty this young city had. The Manhattan skyline, once a phantasmagorical monument to the New World's glory and greed, was, Louie felt, fast coming to resemble one of those sterile geometric *objets* around which rich faggots used to coordinate their décors.

Looking across the Hudson to Jersey City, where he had been born, Louie saw that even there the waterfront was changing. They called it the Jersey City Renaissance. But Louie knew its Medici and its Borgias and its Sforzas from the old days. It was a renaissance of condominiums and kickbacks, ready-mixed concrete and plasterboard walls, glass and aluminum and the cheapest wiring money could buy. None of it would last as long as the pier-pilings that had stood in its place.

Louie turned away from what had changed. He closed his eyes for a moment. The sun still fell on this bench, and the breezes still came.

The rush-hour commotion around him was beginning to wane. He could hear churchbells faintly but sonorously pealing—from Trinity perhaps, or maybe even St. Paul's,

123

or both—and he could hear swallows and thrushes in the trees behind him, gulls in the sky overhead. The morning dew was still in the grass, and the breezes carried its light, clovery perfume through the air. Louie wondered how he could have stayed away for so long from this bench so near.

The breezes began to strengthen and to interweave—the balmy prelude to September wind.

Louie watched a well-dressed young man stride hurriedly by with a briefcase and bundle of papers under one arm. Louie remarked to himself how this young man's fine get-up—slate-gray shadow-stripe suit, white shirt, dark blue tie, and shining black wing-tips—was rendered ludicrous by the homburg hat he wore. Hadn't anyone ever told this punk that nobody under the age of forty should wear a homburg hat, that a baby-faced *guaglione*, like this guy, looked like a real asshole in one? Louie shook his head, watching the young man move quickly on. "Eight hundred dollars' worth of clothes down the fuckin' drain," he mumbled to himself. "These Wall Street punks wanna shake the world, and they don't even know how to dress."

Suddenly, the interweaving river breezes descended on the young man's stride in a whirling frenzy. He stood still for a moment, his head down, his jacket and cuffs flapping this way and that in the playful dervish wind. Then he must have felt that homburg tilting on his head, for his free hand rose toward it in a desperate swipe. But that swipe was too late. His hat was in the air, and his thinning hair blew into his eyes, baring the monkish bald spot the hat had likely been worn to hide. Then the weaving breezes seemed to part and to go their own wild ways. The homburg spun along the ground to the west; and, from under his arm, something of his papery load came blowing east, toward Louie. The young man was oblivious to its escape as he chased after his homburg, fitfully lunging and grabbing the air in its path. The hat skittered on, and the young man after it, growing smaller and smaller in the wake of the wind.

Louie watched what was being blown his way. It was a pamphlet of some kind. The breeze died, and the lull left it on the ground halfway toward him. He looked away from it, his meager curiosity vanished. Then the breeze swelled again, opening that windblown thing, lifting it from the ground. It flew toward his feet, its white pages flapping like wings. It lighted again, then moved closer. Once, twice, it somersaulted, then began to dance, to glide and pirouette with dazzling speed. It was not more than a foot away when, with one last swooning rush, it jumped and clung to Louie's leg with a wild, fluttering embrace. Then, as the breeze stilled to a sigh, it fell.

Louie picked it up and looked at it. It was a prospectus, printed on fancy paper, from the British brokerage firm of G. W. Joynson & Co. It had some nice pictures: an engraving of the Liverpool cotton exchange; sharply detailed color photographs of gold ingots, cotton fresh-burst from its husk, nuggets of lead, lichenlike flakes of copper. He ran his hand over the smooth, rich pages, glanced awhile at the pictures. Then he rolled it into a spyglass and looked through it into the sky.

Earlier that morning, on the other side of the river, Joe Brusher had stood at the drainboard of his kitchen sink squeezing the contents of a large can of Ronsonol lighter fluid into an empty Martell pint bottle.

Now, beneath the grassy ground where Louie sat, his maroon Buick hissed southward through the Brooklyn Battery Tunnel. He parked on Dwight Street, near Van Dyke, then walked to the old warehouses that faced the piers where Dwight Street ended. Joe Brusher disliked this part of South Brooklyn. He disliked its look and its smell and its people, and he always spat when he walked these streets.

He stopped at a narrow three-story building set between two other narrow three-story buildings. These three buildings were in practically identical states of dilapidation. Their windows, two on each floor, were either boarded up or broken. Brittle, flaking patches of dirty gray, the remnants of some long-ago paint job, clung here and there to their crumbling brick facades. But the middle building, the building where Joe Brusher stopped, was distinguished by a relatively new-looking steel door and jambs. Joe Brusher rapped hard on that door, hard enough and loud enough to scatter the gulls and pigeons that were the only visible life around.

A face came to the little wire-reinforced window set into the door. It was the face of a man who was in his forties, but it was a face that appeared much older than that. Its lymphatic pallor was that of a man who was a stranger to natural light and to peaceful sleep. His eyes, red and darkly shadowed, and squinting now through the smoke that rose from the cigar between his teeth, looked like open sores that would not heal.

The door opened halfway, and, around the cigar clenched in its teeth, that dire face spoke: "I'm on my way out here, Joe." It sounded like both an apology and a complaint.

"I ain't a customer, Billy, I'm a messenger."

"Another candygram from Staten Island?"

"Yeah, more or less."

The door opened wider, and Joe Brusher stepped into a small wood-paneled foyer lighted overhead by a bare pink bulb. The man locked the steel door behind them. Beyond the foyer, the entire floor was carpeted in red. The walls were painted pale pink. To the left was a horseshoe-shaped bar with gleaming cash registers set on either side of a well-stocked blue-mirrored partition. Along the opposite wall were three regulation blackjack tables with six seats set at each of them. From the center of the ceiling hung a large fake Tiffany chandelier. As warm as it was outside, the chill in this hollow place was unpleasant. It came not from air-conditioning, but from the foul humidity seeping through the dank sepulchral stone beneath the pink paint and musty red carpeting.

"So, how's business?" Joe Brusher asked offhandedly as he followed the man across the floor toward the open door of a poky room in the back.

"The guy that shapes up for me just left," the man grumbled over his shoulder. "He found three bucks and a ten-dollar chip on the floor. He's doin' better than me."

"Shit, Billy, you took enough of my money in this joint to keep your ass in silk for a hundred years."

The man said nothing; he just kept walking until he reached the little room in the back. In it, there was a desk of sorts—a piece of half-inch plywood anchored to the wall and supported underneath by lengths of two-by-four—on which there was a telephone, an ashtray, and a mess of papers. There was a swivel chair and a coatrack and a file-storage box made of corrugated cardboard and a billy club hanging from a nail behind the door.

The man sat in the swivel chair, relighted his cigar, and shook his head in what was intended to be a show of exhaustion. "So," he said, "whose stupid son-in-law wants to become a blackjack dealer now?"

Joe Brusher, standing there, smiled a little. He pointed to the telephone. "I think you ought to call out there," he said. "He wants me to bring out some papers. Some books, or some shit. I don't know. He'll tell you."

"Papers? What papers?" The man looked at the mess of papers on the desk, and he breathed hard. "What does he want?"

"Ah, Billy, you know me. I don't ask, I just do. Call him, he'll tell you what he wants. I don't like to get involved."

Joe Brusher reached casually into his jacket and took out his Martell bottle. He looked at his watch, then looked at the man, who looked at Joe's bottle, then looked at the phone.

"Want a drink?" Joe Brusher asked.

The man winced disgustedly at the bottle and waved his hand. "I'd shit blood for a week," he said.

Joe Brusher shrugged and uncapped the pint. The man began to dial. Joe Brusher stood the uncapped pint on top of the file-storage box. He took a cigarette from the pack in his pocket and he placed it in his mouth. Then he took a fresh book of matches from that same pocket, reaching across the desk for the ashtray.

Dialing the last digit, the man glanced up as Joe Brusher struck a match. Then he turned again toward the phone. In an instant, realizing that Joe Brusher did not smoke, his eyes shot around again and saw Brusher put the lighted match not to the cigarette in his mouth but to the ashtray in his hand; and he saw the ashtray flare as the open book of matches in it was ignited.

In that stilled moment of his confusion and dismay, the seated man moved the receiver from his ear, and his mouth opened in a trancelike way, then exploded in sound.

"What the fuck—"

"Catch!"

With a long underhand flourishing thrust of the bottle, Joe Brusher doused the man's face and front, and, simultaneously releasing his grip but not the impetus of his thrust, he let the bottle fly into the man's bolting lap. At the same time, into that lap from Joe Brusher's other hand went the ashtray's flaring flame.

The man was up and lunging toward him. His horribly contorted, howling face was little more than two feet from Brusher's eyes when it burst into blue incandescence.

The man's hands, which had grabbed for Joe Brusher's throat, now flailed furiously in the air, slapping and thrashing at himself as the lambent blue fire that played upon him began to ripple and to rise in fluttering tongues of yellowish flame. One hand soon also flared with glowing blue and ruffling gold. The man waved it violently before him, as, with his other hand, he jabbed and pawed at the blinding burning of his eyelids, driving that wild burning deeper into the eyes beneath them with every frantic swipe.

Joe Brusher kicked the heavy swivel chair into the man's shin, jarring him backward in his desperate agony. The stench of scorched flesh and burned hair overtook the smell of the naphtha fumes. Convulsing and roaring before him on the floor, the burning man looked to Joe Brusher like a monstrous embryo aflame. The fire that danced now over every part of him could actually be heard—it was a flapping sound, like that of a wet flag in a low wind—and its heat billowed forth in waves. More and more smoke filled the room as the flames burned deeper, roasting the tallowy flesh beneath the skin; and the soot of the man's incinerated clothing flew through the air like mad black moths.

Joe Brusher took the billy club from behind the door and whacked the man's bared, blistering shoulder. It was like hitting a tightly packed bundle of smoldering papers— fiery cinders of charred skin swirled through the room. The man screamed hideously through black, swollen lips that bled from deep cracks. It was the loudest and most terrible scream that Joe Brusher had ever heard. He brought down the club again, across the skull this time, and the scream-ing ceased with a horrid bleat beneath the crunch of the blow. He dropped the club and backed away in disgust. Strips of blistering skin were crackling loose from the man's bashed head, and the flames were blowing them free like gruesome serpentine streamers. Embers were drifting and lighting throughout the room, kindling tiny blazes everywhere. There was fire in Joe Brusher's cuffs. He smacked it out with a hand that sweated and shook in equal measure.

He bent to retrieve the telephone receiver from the floor where it lay, quickly letting it go with a loud "Damn!" as the heated plastic seared his fingertips. He then raised the receiver by its cord and jimmied it back to its cradle. Tak-ing from the desk the mess of papers, the edges of which were already curling with a slow fire, he looked about for a flame to further ignite them. With another "Damn!" he poked the papers into the fire that burned bright across the spasmodically heaving chest of the dying man. Then with that torch of paper he hurried the spread of the flames throughout that little room. The plywood desk, the cardboard storage boxes, even the phone were set ablaze. He tore off a piece of burning cardboard and carried it with him from the room, tossing it down to the red carpeting. With a frightful *whoosh*, the fire moved across the floor like a burning tide. Joe Brusher, caught off-guard by the velocity of this fuming chemical wildfire, staggered back, then ran.

He pulled hard at the locked door. In that moment, as thick, suffocating smoke began to fill the foyer like a deadly fog, a sudden and chilling dread wrenched his heart. In a flash no less sudden, he remembered entering this door. He saw the doomed man turn a key to lock it behind him, saw the doomed man remove that key and place it in his pocket; saw that doomed man now, burning and laughing, laughing and burning. That fitful, jerking heaving of his chest—it was laughter.

Then his hand was on the bolt-switch, and he was out of that place.

An hour and a half later, lying in a hot bath, he turned that hand slowly before his eyes and stared at it until it ceased to be his own.

On the following morning, in the sunny front parlor of a big house on Castleton Avenue in Staten Island, Joe Brusher extended that hand, and an older man in slippers and a robe put an envelope in it.

"Plant a tree in Israel," he said as he handed it to him.

Joe Brusher counted the money without removing it from the envelope. There were forty hundred-dollar bills and a check made out to him for three thousand dollars. In the lower left-hand corner of the check were written the words HOUSE PAINTING. He tucked the envelope into his jacket pocket with a trace of disappointment in his breath. He had been hoping for a little something extra.

"You did good," the man said, easing himself into an armchair. As he sat, his robe drooped open, exposing his boxer shorts—they seemed to match the wallpaper in this room—and pale spindly legs. "You see the *News* this morning?"

Joe Brusher shook his head in oblique distaste.

"'Gambling War in Brooklyn,'" the man mocked with a golden-toothed grin. "They bought it lock, stock, and barrel. The Jew lightnin', Joe, that's what made it look good. The paper said the cops called it a—what the fuck was it—a..."

This guy's ready for a fuckin' E.E.G., Joe Brusher's inner voice mumbled as the man squinted gropingly toward the ceiling.

"'Detectives said the killing and arson were a new volley in the war to control illegal gambling in Brooklyn.' Yeah, that was it. That's what the paper said." The man scratched his chest through his undershirt. "So, Joe," he said, "tell me. How'd that little rat cunt-eater go when he went? How'd he check out?"

"You had to be there."

"But he suffered." It was a question expressed as a statement.

"Yeah," Joe Brusher said, not wanting to show his impatience or his disquietude. "He suffered." He thought of the previous morning and of the little something extra that he had not found in the envelope. "It wasn't too pretty there yesterday in that joint."

The man sensed the note of umbrage in Joe Brusher's voice. He nodded aloofly, disdainfully.

"You're getting dainty in your old age, Joe? You're a fucking floral arranger all of a sudden now?"

"Look, this was different." The words had an angry weight to them.

"*Different*," the man said, sneering.

"Yeah, different. I coulda dropped that bastard in ten seconds. This was a major fuckin' production."

"It's what I wanted."

"It's what you wanted. So you got it."

"Watch it, Giusepp'."

Joe Brusher sat there, and he breathed deeply, and he told himself that September was now here and that its third Monday soon enough would come, and that then he would be free, forever, of cocksuckers such as this.

"You know, Joe"—the man's voice was subdued now, and his tone was almost avuncular—"it's like the philosopher says: Count your blessings."

Joe Brusher pursed his lips and nodded slowly as if in reflective cognizance of the wisdom not only of those words but of the man who uttered them as well. And the man perceived this to be good.

The morning sky was darkening. Driving back to Jersey across the Bayonne Bridge, Joe Brusher watched the first, misty drops of a late-summer rain splash and softly spatter on his windshield. He remembered a song called "September in the Rain." He had heard it long ago, a lifetime ago, drifting from a seaside bandshell through the starry rifts of a nighttime boardwalk under which he lay with his cock in the mouth of his best friend's little sister. He would have sung it now, but he couldn't remember the words.

A t about ten that night, Louie poured himself a drink and, looking about for something to read, sat down with what the breeze had blown him in Battery Park.

The prospectus detailed something called the Computer Managed Technical Trading System. For the sum of five thousand pounds, it was explained, one could become part of a commodities-trading syndicate managed by computer under the direction of the venerable British brokerage house of G. W. Joynson & Co., Ltd. Programmed to monitor and analyze the daily price movements in seven London-based commodity markets—copper, tin, lead, zinc, coffee, cocoa, and sugar—the computer nimbly spat out trading commands unhindered by "any emotional considerations which often cause profit to be taken too quickly." In addition to management charges, a "performance fee" of twenty percent was extracted from all profits exceeding a certain level.

Louie quietly grinned. "Performance fee," of course, was just another way of saying "vig." Whether it was an old chewed-up lead pencil or an eight-million-dollar computer; whether the man holding the purse strings wore a dirty T-shirt or Egyptian cotton and a Sulka tie; whether it was Bishopsgate or the corner of Carmine Street, the Bank of England or *la materassa*—whatever it was, wherever it was, however it was said, it all came down to vig.

He closed the handsome booklet and tossed it aside, but the thoughts it had roused stayed with him. He took a sip and he closed his eyes.

All his life, from boyhood, he had read newspapers. He remembered the defunct *Daily Mirror*, with its pages and pages and pages devoted to the mystery of Mario Lanza's death. He remembered the *Post* before it became a half-assed racing sheet for two-dollar bettors. Every day—except Sunday: too much paper, too much bullshit—he read either the *Daily News* or the *Times*, often both. Even when he was on a bat, he at least usually checked out the *News*, using the Word Jumble to objectively gauge his drunkenness. (If he failed to unscramble the first two words in the time it took him to smoke a cigarette, he knew that he should enter into no business dealings that day.) And, on more weekdays than not, he also read the *Wall Street Journal*. He liked it because there were no photographs.

He was not proud of this daily paper-reading. In a way, it was—like smoking cigarettes, like drinking coffee, like watching television, like masturbating, like carrying his own shopping bags—a part of the gray aspect of his existence. Unlike those other activities, however, it had its lasting rewards. Through the years, he had been kept abreast of, and attuned to, the endless, exundant flow of meaninglessness in which fools perceived meaning. He had been kept apprised of his lifetime's blinking glimpse of the eternal sameness-in-flux in which fools descried the illusory glimmerings of newness. He had learned that only the faces and names of the politicians, of the stars, of the killers and the killed, changed from day to day and from year to year, and that, even then, the faces changed not much at all. He had learned things that he could not recall learning, information that was as useless as it was unforgettable.

In youth, he had watched his elders pore over "Ching Chow" in the *Daily News*. This little cartoon, which occupied a two-by-three-inch space every day near the racing charts, was believed by many of those elders to contain the key to the next winning Brooklyn number. By counting the buttons on Ching Chow's mandarin jacket, by noting how many of his fingers were extended and in which direction they pointed, by adding and subtracting blades of grass or the drawn lines of this or that, by studying Ching Chow's aphorism of the day—by these and assorted other hermeneutic methods, people sought to decipher the secret information they believed was hidden there daily. In retrospect, it was always there: If 321 was the winning Brooklyn number, a look back at that morning's "Ching Chow" surely would reveal three buttons, two pointing fingers, and a lone bird flying overhead. If the number was 749, a look back—discounting, of course, the buttons, fingers, and bird—would reveal seven pebbles, four sunrays, and nine words in the aphorism. It was widely held that this secret information was conveyed to the artist by an unknown but actual Chinaman who had grown fabulously wealthy from his occult knowledge of numbers and who now, in his old age, wished to impart that knowledge in his own inscrutable way. To this day, Louie still saw them, though they were fewer now, the old ladies who bought or borrowed the *News* and—before turning to the obituaries, the Italian gossip column, so dear to their hearts—opened directly to "Ching Chow."

But Louie knew things about "Ching Chow" that no one else seemed to know. He knew that Ching Chow had originated before the Brooklyn number, in a Sidney Smith comic strip called "The Gumps." He knew that Captain Peterson, the founder of the *News*, had given Smith a Cadillac as a gift, and that Smith, driving drunk one night through Ohio, in 1947, wrapped the Cadillac around a tree and was killed. He knew that Smith's assistant, Stanley Link, had then taken over "Ching Chow," which by that time had been removed from "The Gumps" to its own space. He knew that Link had died in 1956, and that, since then, "Ching Chow" had been done by Henri Arlen, the same guy who did the Word Jumble. He knew that Arlen —who snipped off Ching Chow's pigtail—did not even play the numbers, and that he derived many of Ching Chow's aphorisms from Shakespeare. And he knew that the greatest public uproar in the history of the *News* was when "Ching Chow" inadvertently was left out one day.

These were the sort of things he could not recall learning, the sort of information he could neither use nor forget. How had he come to know these things, which he was convinced he had never read? Had they accrued to his mind, a few words here, a glimpse there, building up over the years, particle by particle, like the gradual, imperceptible increase of dust upon the surface of any idle object? To dwell on questions such as these, Louie realized, would be to set sail truly for the farthest Thule of uselessness.

But there were other sorts of information, other layers of dust gathered in the course of gray time. While perhaps just as meaningless, this other information was of a plainly more useful nature.

The financial pages were as familiar to him as the sports section and the funnies. He followed them every bit as habitually as he followed "Ching Chow," and with the same droll fascination. He knew that people looked to these pages for the same reason people looked to "Ching Chow" —to find the key of gold. It was true that those who sought the key by calculating economic indicators, interest rates, and price indexes usually had less dirt under their nails and smelled better than those who calculated buttons, blades of grass, and pebbles. But, in the end, it was all Chinese arithmetic. People read the words of so-called financial experts with the same eager credulity with which others read the words—the far wiser words—of Ching Chow. Did it never occur to those people, Louie often wondered, that if any of these prescient experts knew what he was talking about he would not need to peddle his expertise to newspapers for a lousy few hundred a week? Buy gold when inflation rises, the experts proclaimed. Play 660 when you dream of gold, the dreambooks advised. The difference between these divinations was only one of seeming sophistication. Financial writers and racing handicappers, as far as Louie could see, used the same crystal ball. It was fortunate for them that, as every storefront gypsy knew, suckerdom was vast.

Louie paid as little mind to the financial writers as he paid to the buttons on Ching Chow's jacket. For him, the numbers—numbers of every kind—were what it all came down to, be it the Brooklyn number contained in the daily track handle at the bottom of the racing charts or the Dow Jones Industrial Average in the stock-market-index charts. A daily number—any daily number—was, for Louie, like the weather. He wanted to know what it was, even if he had no intention of venturing into it.

Though he had never been involved in a financial transaction that had taken place above street level, he had watched, day in and day out, the changing currents of foreign-exchange rates, bonds and notes, stocks and options. In early 1975, when gold had gone on sale for a hundred and ninety-something an ounce, he had figured it to be a good buy, in that it would, in its tangible, gleaming simplicity, appeal to, and create a rising demand among, that lowest common denominator of greedy cocksuckers, those benighted masses who only understood what they could put in their pockets. Most people, he thought, would not look twice at a bearer-bond coupon lying in the street, but they would run through traffic and lightning to get at a twelve-dollar gold-plated earring.

But, at the time, he had had barely enough money to

drink and gamble, let alone to invest. He still shook his head when he thought what could have been if he had laid aside just two grand to put where his mouth was that winter. Buying either a couple of gold certificates or a single, hundred-ounce gold futures contract on margin, parlaying as he went along, he could have made a small fortune in six years' time.

Fortune had lifted her skirts again in the spring of 1982, when the price of platinum, having risen to over a grand an ounce, fell to barely a quarter of that. Louie was convinced that the price of platinum, which had dropped then beneath the price of gold for the first time, would soon again ascend to its traditional premium over the commoner metal. Less than a year later, it did; and, after that, it continued to rise.

There was no excuse for him that time. There had been money enough stashed away beneath his refrigerator—almost five grand. But he had chosen not to buy platinum. Instead, following a baser instinct and viewing fortune through an evil eye, he had chosen to put his money on the street. There, instead of enriching him, as his evil eye had forseen it would, it was all but eaten by the moths of perfidy, and by the rats.

But his evil eye, like his earlier lack of money, could not be blamed alone. There had been intimidation at work. Comfortable as he was among numbers, the actual marketplace, which in turns made and was swayed by those numbers, somehow daunted him. Though he would not admit it aloud, he felt that marketplace to be somewhat beyond his class.

This, he now came to see, was an absurdity. As a boy, beneath the shadow of the cross of Trinity Church, he had sold dope to the men and women of that marketplace. Many of them were twice as old as he, and most of them never even knew they were being beat. He had sold them more oregano than his grandmother had bought in a lifetime, and they had come back for more. He had colored saccharin tablets purple with a felt-tipped marker. They had bought them from him, swallowed them, and seen God.

The new chairman of the Commodity Exchange, Louie reflected, was younger than he. Had he known enough to buy gold in 1975, platinum in 1982? Had he ever read "Ching Chow"? All the *Times* said was that he liked opera and played a fair game of tennis.

And, behind Louie's eyes, there passed the image of that young man awkwardly chasing his ludicrous homburg through the laughing wind.

Louie went into the bedroom, to his pants that hung from a nail by the closet. From a pocket of those pants, he took a nickel and he tossed it lightly with a spin into the air. It hit the floor. He bent and saw the look of smug determination on Thomas Jefferson's leftward-gazing profile. From a dresser drawer, he dug out four red plastic dice. Hunkering, he shook them in his cupped hands, then cast them tumbling toward the wallboard. They bounced to a rest, and he counted the white spots facing upward.

On the day before he was to take over for Giacomo, Louie went to Newark.

Something inside him, something beneath the skin or something the breeze had breathed into him, steered him there. More and more frequently in his recent brooding, the image of the old man's face had drifted in and out of his mind. Though he knew that face almost as well as he knew his own, it had grown strangely unclear in these recent visitations, its features and expressions shifting uncannily, hazily, as through a mist in darkness.

Only now, as he walked through downtown Newark under a sun hidden by clouds the color of noxious smoke, did he finally apprehend what had brought him here. He wanted to see that face. He wanted to see if it was a stranger's face. He wanted to see what was written on it; wanted somehow to confirm or to resolve the feelings that his last trip to Newark had sown; wanted somehow to know if this vague, abiding fortuity of the blood, this kinship, was a curse or a dream or a blessing. He wanted to know.

He turned the corner to Halsey Street. There sat Ernie on his folding chair, his familiar shillelagh in his hand. He peered at Louie from under the brim of a baseball cap.

Louie had turned this corner countless times to see

Ernie sitting by the door of the narrow building where his uncle lived; and every one of those countless times, Ernie had broken into a broad, warm smile upon recognizing him. This time, there was no smile.

"Good to see you, Lou."

And there was no warmth.

"Good to see you, Ernie."

Ernie nodded absently, as if in subdued reflection of this abundant goodness. Louie watched him nod, and then he nodded, too.

"You look like you're a thousand miles away."

"Nah," the older man said softly, glancing off, avoiding Louie's eyes. "Contemplatin' the late double at Saratoga, that's all."

Louie watched the black man's fingers fidget at the knotted crook of the shillelagh. This was not the Ernie he knew.

Louie unlocked the heavy steeled oak door and moved into the cool, dim silence beyond it. His eyes turned to the little painting in the pine-molding frame, that odd picture of trees and lake which had haunted him in his youth, and which the years had transformed into indistinct, dark-hued shadows of gloom and foreboding. He stared at it, trying to remember what it had looked like twenty-five years ago and more, when he had first seen it, when it first had filled him with alternate feelings of enchantment and dread. Narrowing his eyes, he began to see it as it then had been. The tenebrous pines, the unnaturally still, murky water—they never had been clear. They had been painted as if seen through a veil of mourning, or through a mysterious haze that seemed to blend the suffusing, luminous glow of heaven with the falling darkness of death. It was the mist through which he had seen his uncle's face.

He put his hand on the banister, and he ascended the creaking stairs. He knocked twice, then waited.

"Well, well, well, as the ditch-digger said to the snake, if it ain't my long-lost nephew."

The son of a bitch is drunk, Louie thought. He could smell the booze on his breath from two feet away.

But the smell of liquor came from a lone shot of brandy the old man had just finished; and the bottle had been promptly returned to the cupboard. No, Louie saw, he was not loaded. He was merely happy. Off his rocker maybe, senile at last, Louie thought fleetingly as he beheld his uncle's shit-eating grin; off his rocker, but nevertheless happy.

"You must have extrasensory deception, kid. I was just sitting here thinking about you, and here you are. Ain't life a bitch."

Louie followed him to the big comfortable chairs by the window. Happy or not, he observed, his uncle appeared visibly frailer and shuffled more slowly than when Louie had last seen him.

"That was some lamb, pal. *Che capretto.* I roasted it with garlic and wine, lived off it for a week. I even got Ernie to break down and try the *capozell'* this time. I was after him for years, but he always said it gave him the willies. I gave him the *gota*, the cheek meat. He loved it. He still wouldn't touch the eyes, though. That was all right by me. They're the best part. I save 'em for last." Holding on to the arms of the chair, he let his ass down slowly. "Where'd you get that lamb, anyway?"

"The children's zoo at Central Park."

The old man's shit-eating grin returned, and his ample belly and sunken chest moved with a deep, soundless laugh.

Louie studied the old man's face. As far as he could tell, the old man was sincerely happy. It was as if he had been newly relieved of some great weight. His look—clear and unshifting and not a stranger's—seemed as open and as receptive as it had, on that spring day not too long ago, seemed evasive and estranged. Yet there was an untellable something still in the air—an untellable, unknowable, unseeable something that pervaded the air where the vectors of this gleaming black telephone, Il Capraio, a man called Joe Brusher, and his uncle converged.

"Speaking of Ernie," Louie ventured, "I just ran into him downstairs. He didn't seem to be himself."

Uncle John nodded slowly, agreeing with his nephew's observation but not approving of it.

"Who knows what goes through people's minds?" he said. "That's one thing you can never do, get inside another man's mind. Hell, many's the time I saw you, even without my cheaters on, you looked like you were ready to check out. It was like talking to a damn sphinx, trying to talk to you. Then you were hunky-dory again. It passed. Everything passes. You could probably say the same about me. In spades."

"I guess that's true enough," Louie remarked, still watching the old man's face, and seeing nothing but the uncle he had always known.

"Anyhow, like I said, I was just sittin' here thinking about you before."

"I been thinkin' about you, too."

"Yeah?" The old man's chest and belly began to move again in silent laughter. "We sound like two fags in a piano bar."

"I been busy, that's all."

"That's what I figured, Lou. But I started wondering. Another few days, I was maybe going to get on the old horn here." He raised his eyebrows, smiling, gesturing toward the telephone on the table between them.

"That would've been somethin'," Louie snorted, "gettin' a phone call from you." He looked at it, that enigmatic black presence. "I never thought I'd see the day."

"Well, you know, Lou, it's like the guy on the TV says,

you got to move with the times. Next I get the little *come-si-chiama* with the beeper for my belt, the Dick Tracy wristwatch, the hi-fi earmuffs, the works."

"You know, Unc, you got a good shot at becomin' the world's oldest living ballbuster. Most guys your age, they just sort of roll over and start suckin' up to Jesus. You don't quit. You just keep right on bustin' 'em."

The old man snorted faintly, his eyes wandering to those familiar shadows across the room. Louie lighted a cigarette.

"So," he said, "read any good dollar bills lately?"

Giovanni did not respond. Slowly, in the silence, as Louie watched the smoke from his cigarette furl in the light that beamed through the lace, impatience swelled inside him. At last, he rapped hard with his knuckles on that black enigma that sat between them. The old man turned suddenly, looking at it as if it had rung. Then he looked at Louie.

"For once and for all," Louie said, "what the fuck is going on here? What is this?" He was gesturing to the telephone, but the angry tone of his question ranged further.

"It's a goddamn telephone," Giovanni said sternly, "like you have, like damn near everybody else in this world has." Then his voice cooled. "A man gets old, he starts to feel alone."

"Is that what the guy on TV says?"

There was something then like a heavy trigger being cocked in the hot, still air.

"What about the passport?"

Louie's knowledge of the passport seemed to surprise the old man, but he concealed it well.

"You don't have one?" he countered.

"I have one."

"I know you do. You showed it to me once. Where'd you go with it?"

"Nowhere."

"Where you going?"

"Nowhere."

"Well?"

The old man's chin jutted out. He looked straight ahead and raised his palms, as if, having concluded an irrefutable argument of great eloquence, he awaited the roaring approval of the Roman Senate.

Each looked away from the other, and they let the tide of silence rise awhile, until it was almost as if what had been said had not been said.

"This kind of weather always makes me think of when I was a kid," the old man remarked softly.

Louie could not envision his great-uncle as a kid. In Louie's mind, he was never young; he was just there, as he was now.

"The last days of summer. It always seemed to be the last days of summer in that little town."

The little town was Casalvecchio di Puglia. Louie had grown up hearing tales of that far-off place. The teller of those tales was his grandfather, a man who seemed to smile when everyone else was mad and seemed to be mad when everyone else was smiling. It was an *albanese* hill town, high up in Apulia, near Italy's spur, his grandfather told him; on a clear day, it seemed that you could see the world, and if the breeze was right, piss down upon it. Louie had always thought of it as a place where the eyes were everybody's favorite part of a meal.

"Ah," the old man sighed, as if he regretted having disturbed the silence with his words. Or, Louie thought, as if he regretted ever having left that far-off place.

The old man drew a deep, peaceful breath. "Anyway," he said, "I told you I've been thinking about you. I wanted you to have this."

Louie watched the old man slowly and with difficulty twist the big diamond ring free from his gnarled finger. He saw it come off, and he saw the circle of pale flesh it bared.

Then it lay warm and heavy in the hollow of his own hand. He put it on his finger, and when he looked up, he saw something he had never seen. There was a tear in the old man's eye.

Nothing more of consequence was said between them that day. They talked awhile of the baseball season that was nearing its end; and they talked of the weather's changing, of the waning length of the days and the sweet smoky scent that would soon be in the breeze. The fall had always been their favorite time of year.

Beneath their talk, Louie's sense of bewilderment still stirred. The immense gift of the ring, far from quelling his confusion, had only increased it. The light in its gleam was not the light he sought, and it was not the light he had lost. It was the glow of his own anger, the glow of old ways that both swayed him and enraged him. He looked at his uncle, and he followed his uncle's eyes to the shadows across the room.

He descended the stairs toward the light of day, not turning to look at the picture on the wall—he had no way of knowing that he would never see it again. He shook his head, and with his right hand he seemed to wave away the world.

The bar on Central Avenue was windowless, a place where sunlight never shone. Day or night, it was a darkness unto itself.

Facing Ernie in the booth was a slender young black man with yellow eyes, yellow teeth, glistening marceled hair, and a pencil-thin mustache. A crescentlike scar, the color of old copper, ran across the front of his neck, from one jugular vein to the other. He was leaning back, blowing Kool smoke toward the half-finished vodka-and-soda on the table before him.

"Black or white?" he asked.

"White," Ernie said.

"How old?"

"Like the hills."

The young man nodded pensively.

"What about the noise? It's the blast from that damn shotgun that worries me."

The young man snorted and waved his hand. "Believe me," he said, "that's the least of our problems."

I n the dead of night, in that black-curtained place on the Street of Silence, Il Capraio sat at his little table near the wall and looked into Joe Brusher's eyes.

"Fifty grand is a lot of money," he said.

"And the two million and change it's gonna buy is a hell of a lot more money," Joe Brusher said.

"I know that. I just wanna be sure that everything goes right."

"Frank, you worry too much. Even the fuckin' doctor tells you that."

"And another thing, Joe. Don't call it 'change.' I don't like that. Three hundred and seventy-five grand ain't change. It ain't change to nobody in this world, least of all to a guy who goes around borrowin' fifties. Now, let me hear you say it right. What does that fifty grand buy?"

"Two million, three hundred and seventy-five thousand dollars," he said. And a slug through your rotten fucking brain and two up your asshole, he added inwardly.

"And as far as you're concerned, you don't think glommin' his take is gonna be any problem?"

"One through the head, two up the ass. That usually solves the problem."

Joe Brusher stood, and he walked to the small bar and poured himself a drink. He tasted it, then returned with it to the table.

"What are you gonna do with all that money, Joe? You think about that yet?"

Joe Brusher shrugged; then he drew a long breath through his nostrils. "Dope," he said. "I think I might go that route. Set up a few spics, get one of them guys from out on the Island to watch over 'em, lay back for a while. The good life. That's what I'm gonna buy with that money, Frank, the good life. Like that shine says in that commercial: 'Because it's *my* money.'"

Il Capraio nodded sagaciously.

"I don't think you'd go wrong there, Joe. A guy your age, still young, dope's a good thing. You got a market that never goes down, it only goes up.

"Me, I think they should legalize the shit. I think they should sell it in fuckin' candy stores like Life Savers and chewin' gum. Five dollars of the shit ain't worth fifty cents. They could sell it for a buck and make more money than R. J. Reynolds makes sellin' tobacco. These jerk-off kids want it, let 'em have it. That way, your streets would be fuckin' safe again, and we'd get rid of all the scum we got. They'd stay where they belong and kill themselves with the shit, and the world would be a better place."

"That makes a lot of sense, Frank. But laws don't make sense. Lawyers don't want to end crime. It'd put them outa business. They got a vested interest in dope, just like doctors got a vested interest in cancer, like undertakers got a vested interest in death. It's their bread and butter. That's why I don't think they'll ever make dope legal. It'd solve too many problems. And it'd take a lot of money out of a lot of fancy-ass pockets."

"You're probably right, Joe. Either way, I don't think either of us'll live to see the day when it is legal. That's why I say, for a guy like you, still young, dope's a good thing."

"And what about you, Frank? What are you gonna do with your two million and...three hundred and seventy-five thousand?"

"Ah, Joe, I'm an old man. I outlived what little family I had. I don't drink, I don't gamble. I only use my prick to piss. If my prostate gets any worse, I won't even be usin' it much for that. Someday, Joe, you'll understand. At my age, money's different. It's nice just to know you got it. It's like goin' to church. It makes you feel good."

Joe Brusher put forth his lower lip and nodded as if in rumination of Il Capraio's words. Then Il Capraio waved his hand.

"But let's just get it first, eh? There'll be time enough to count it after that."

It was a little after three o'clock in the morning when Louie passed the lighted slit of those black curtains, walking alone to Giacomo's joint with the key to the lock in his fist.

Giacomo had left the joint clean—as clean as it ever was, anyway. Louie turned on the light in the back. He switched on the air conditioner, plugged in the jukebox, and put on a pot of coffee. He turned on the radio (set, as ever, to New York's regulation low-life drinking frequency, WNEW-AM), then the ice machine. Reaching beneath it, he removed the cashbox and counted what was there: a hundred singles, forty fives, twenty tens, ten twenties, and eight rolls of quarters. He wrote these figures down on a slip of paper, put the money in the open drawer of the busted cash register, put the slip of paper in the box, and put the box back under the ice machine. Then he poured himself a cup of coffee, sat with it at the end of the bar, lighted a cigarette, and waited.

His first customer was a familiar old man with the rather improbable name of Goo-Goo Mangiacavallo. He was, and he always had been, the best dresser Louie knew. He was a man who had three worsted-wool herringbone topcoats—dark gray, midnight blue, and black—and two cashmere overcoats, a beige and a blue. Like his dozen suits—and he was never seen without a suit and tie—

those coats were made for him, lined in silk and embroidered with an elegant, majuscule *M* on their inside pockets, away from the eyes of the world.

Louie immediately recognized the tilt of his fedora coming through the door, from darkness into dimness.

"Luigi, my friend," proclaimed Goo-Goo in his deep nicotine baritone. "Long time, no see."

Louie smiled. He was happy to have Goo-Goo as his first customer, rather than some drunken pain-in-the-ass from God-knew-where.

Goo-Goo sat down next to Louie. He adjusted his tie and his cuffs and his hearing-aid.

Louie got up and fixed him a Canadian Club and soda. It was the only thing he ever knew him to drink. Goo-Goo had placed a crisp twenty-dollar bill on the bar.

Louie had always found Goo-Goo's money to be even more impressive than his clothes. It was not the quantity of his money that Louie found impressive—true though it was that Goo-Goo freely spent more than most. Rather, it was the newness of his money. Louie had never seen Goo-Goo put up a bill that did not seem to be in mint condition. He seemed to use only virgin money, and to shun currency that had been handled by the unwashed, the unmonogrammed. He had always been this way about money, Louie was told. Long ago, during Prohibition, when Goo-Goo had sold alcohol in gallon-size olive-oil cans, he was known behind his back as *Nettidollari*—Cleanbucks—and it was rumored in those days that, every Saturday night, he had his spinster sister iron his money for him along with his laundry. All Louie knew for sure was that Goo-Goo was a gentleman.

"Eggs and *pancetta* I had this mornin', Lou. Toast and jelly, nice cuppa tea."

He brought his fingertips together, raised them to his lips, and kissed them. Then he leaned back, took out his pack of Luckies, put one in his mouth, and lighted it.

"What the hell time do you go to bed at night, Goo-Goo?"

"Eight o'clock. It gets dark, I go to bed. I wake up. I eat. I take a shave. I get dressed. I come out. I do what I gotta do. I have my few. I get undressed. I eat. I go to bed. I wake up. I eat—"

"I get the picture, Goo-Goo."

"Stayin' up after dark ain't natural. That's how people get cancer. It puts your whole system on the fritz. That's why you got all these *finocch's* today, all these fairies. They were conceived after dark. In the old days, you didn't have that. A man and wife went to bed early in them days. Then they came along with the TV, the go-go, this, that, the other thing. Next thing you know, you got fruits all over the place. I mean, two and two is four. You don't gotta be no Einstein to figure this shit out."

"And you never went to college or anything?" Louie asked, looking at him sideways.

"Fuck no."

Slowly, a few at a time, the early regulars started to arrive: bartenders and bouncers and waitresses who were on their roundabout way home from work. Most of them knew Louie, and he knew them. As a rule, they were good trade. Like most people in the business, they tipped well, did not order silly-ass drinks, and did not much play the jukebox.

Then, drunk unto drooling, there entered a famous actor from these parts, a man of about forty who had long ago forgotten his friends and had, in turn, been forgotten by them. He took a chair near Goo-Goo.

"Out slummin', Hollywood?" Goo-Goo asked him.

The famous actor uttered a sound that was lost between a laugh and a snort, and he patted Goo-Goo on the back. He took out a hundred-dollar bill and placed it on the bar. Louie looked at it; then he looked at the famous actor and he shook his head.

"You and these fuckin' hundreds again," he said.

"It's all I got, Lou."

"Cab drivers don't make change anymore?"

"They gave me the limo tonight."

"Limos, hundred-dollar bills. What the fuck is this, 'Lifestyles of the Rich and Famous'? If I knew, I would've lined up a cigarette girl and got a guy to stand around in the shit-house with a towel over his arm."

"I guess you don't want my autograph, huh?"

Louie grinned crookedly and tossed a damp bar rag down on the bar in front of him.

"Well, what is it, movie star? Should I chill the champagne crystal or what?"

"Give me a Martell. And give Mr. Mangiacavallo here whatever he wants. And you, too, my adoring fan."

"I'd rather have the cash," Louie said over his shoulder, walking away.

He returned with a glass of Martell and change for the hundred. The famous actor's eyes were starting to close. Louie banged the drink down to rouse him.

"I took out for Goo-Goo," he said. Then he winked to Goo-Goo: "When you're ready, pal."

And in walked a big fat Irishman whom Louie despised. Wherever this Irishman went, Louie thought, he seemed bent on establishing himself as the loudest, cheapest, stupidest cocksucker in the joint. He was known to Louie only as Grogan—a dank, peaty donkey-shit dollop of a name that seemed to fit him perfectly.

"Give us a taste of mother's milk here, stranger. Your promptness may be rewarded by a shiny dime, coin of the realm," he bellowed, turning with a fool's grin to scan the faces around him, as if anticipating laughter and applause.

Louie put a can of Budweiser in front of him and took his money. He wondered idly if Donna Lou's father had been one of these Grogan-men.

Then came the herd.

There were old faces and there were new faces. The new ones, usually led here by the older ones—who just a few years ago had been new themselves—were mostly in their twenties. Believing themselves to have passed from youth and callowness to the farther side of worldliness, they reeled from the exhilaration of their delusion. Cocky and giddy and declamatory, they had not yet been dealt their humbling blows. Until those blows came, they would remain as they were, thinking that they did not sound like little cunt-eating punks, that they did not look like little cunt-eating punks, and that they were not little cunt-eating punks. And until those blows came, they would be a pain in the ass, here, and wherever they went.

They were bad drinkers and they were bad tippers. Either they asked for ridiculous mixed drinks—Blue Skies, Alabama Slammers, Kirs—and made petulant whining sounds when told that such drinks were not served here, or they drank what they considered to be manly drinks—shots of tequila, or Jack Daniel's—and ended up puking through their noses in mid-affectation. And, no matter how much they talked about money, they threw around quarters like manhole covers, and their idea of a big tip was two bucks on New Year's Eve.

The cocaine creeps, on the other hand, often tipped very well. Flaunting money, rather than just talking about it, was part of their particular delusion. Yet, in their way, they were just as big a pain in the ass as the other punks. They were here now, too, gathering in clusters in the back, near the toilet door.

The crowd was two-deep at the bar, jostling and weaving and hollering and crying and fighting and laughing. Louie, pouring four drinks at a time, glanced down the end of the bar and smiled to see Goo-Goo sitting there aloof and dignified amid the turbulence. Beside him, the famous actor slept, still as stone, as the jukebox behind him blared the noise of somebody even more famous than he.

"Don't you just love Springsteen?"

Louie turned. The girl who had spoken to him was moving her shoulders to the sound of the blare. She was barely twenty, he surmised, not old enough to drink in any legal joint. She had short brown hair and big, ripe breasts that shook as she moved her shoulders. Louie did not know her from Eve, but he remembered making her the Kahlúa-and-cream she held in her hand.

"Yeah," he said. "Good old Bruce. I got all his records. Usually I wear the little rag around the head like him and everything. These days, with Liberace dead and all, Bruce is all that's left."

He walked away to serve another young woman, one he recognized from the old days. She had three different and distinct personalities, this woman: haughty, whorish, and demented. On her left breast, above the lacy line of her brassiere, visible now as he remembered it, there was a tattoo of a crown of thorns encircling the letters *PMS*.

"Louis, dear," she said in her haughtiest voice, "this is my new friend, Hans." She gestured daintily to the bearded mooncalf who sat with her. "Hans is from Denmark," she added, as if it somehow might be of interest to Louie, or to anyone. Upon hearing her words, Hans livened.

"Denmark, yes. I come to New York to make the art. You like the art?" he asked eagerly.

"I like the art."

"I *love* the art," Hans said, glancing furtively to Louie's crotch. "I think here the people, they understand the art. What do you think?"

"I think you were conceived in the dark."

There was a violent shout from halfway down the bar. Louie spun around.

"Get the fuck *away* from me!" the girl who loved Spring-steen was yelling to a tall, hulking, vaguely Hispanic crea-ture that loomed over her.

"What's going on here?" Louie demanded.

"This creep keeps rubbin' his dick against me," the girl loudly complained.

There was laughter in the distance. Nearer, Grogan re-coiled in Hibernian horror.

"I ain't rub no dick 'gainst no one, man. This chick's crazy. I just be standin', mind m'own business, drink my drink." He affected a posture of statuesque innocence. "Like so."

"He's fulla shit!" the girl snarled. "I had my hand on my leg, and he started pressin' right up against it."

"Oh, man!" the looming man wailed in melodramatic disbelief.

"And it was little!" the girl yelled with venomous glee.

The looming man's eyes opened wide, and he seemed about to erupt, or to melt. Louie threw up his hands, then brought them down upon the bar.

"That's enough of this shit," he declared. "You"—he pointed with a gun-barrel forefinger to the looming man—"you want to stay, move away from her." And when the looming man moved, Louie aimed that same forefinger at the girl and lowered his voice. "And you," he said, "you're not even old enough to drink, so don't make waves."

"If I'm a good girl, will you give me a lollipop?" she asked with a naughty pout.

Now Louie remembered what he liked about this job.

"You don't mind getting sticky?" he said with a crooked grin.

"Oh, no," she purred. "I just love getting sticky."

She smiled as Louie poured her another drink. Then the smile faded when he took her money.

As he stepped away, he could hear Grogan trying to start a conversation with her.

"I had my eyes on that guy before, that guy who was botherin' you," the Irishman said. "I was ready to let him have it. If I hit him, he'd never get up. That's why I was tryin' to play it cool."

Some of the cocaine ghouls had drifted to the bar for drinks. To Louie, it always had seemed that these characters tended to drink in colors, that they were more concerned with the tint of a drink than with its taste or contents. From vodka-and-cranberry to vodka-and-orange to vodka-and-grapefruit to green crème de menthe and so on through the noxious gamut of chemically dyed Leroux liqueurs, they traversed the spectrum in their drinking. Tonight, Louie discovered, the trend among them was toward pink: vodka with cranberry *and* grapefruit. Recalling the bottle of Praline Liqueur he had stuck Giacomo with last spring, and realizing that it was gone, it occurred to him that, to Giacomo's chagrin, there must have been an unexpected run on beige sometime during the summer.

Even through the blare of the jukebox, Louie could hear their breathing—a deathly choir of cocaine-congested gasps, loud and convulsive as a drunkard's snoring. And he could smell them, too; for their sweat was not the sweat of humanity. It did not seep, clear and salty, through their skin, but clogged their pores like a fetid, gummy residue, giving them viscid, waxen complexions. Many of them, the ones who were the farthest gone, looked like cadavers awaiting the cosmetician's touch. And yet they gabbled on.

Their flesh and their unnatural memphitic scent was part of what made them seem to Louie like vampires. But, above all, it was their eyes and their mouths that made him think of the devouring undead. It was the way their eyes dwelt on the flesh of others—not so much with sexual longing, but with a preternatural hunger to consume and to merge with that flesh. Their pale, parched lips seemed to crave that same unspeakable sustenance—that moisture of the soul that they seemed desperate to suck through the flesh of others into themselves.

Things Louie heard these cocaine cadavers say corroborated these strange impressions. "I don't enjoy fucking," one of them once told him in the course of a babblesome account of why he and his girlfriend had parted; "I like to *make love* to a woman." And when he spoke those words, the cadaver's vacant eyes seemed to glow, like the eyes of a child at a lactating breast, and he ran his bloated tongue over his dried, puffy lips.

That same man was standing at the bar now. In the moment that Louie glanced his way, a drop of dark crimson dripped from one of his nostrils into the pink drink he was raising to his mouth. Then, suddenly, blood streamed from both his nostrils, drenching his thick mustache and spattering his shirt. He did not panic, but, tilting back his head, merely called for paper towels and some ice.

From the other end of the bar, the woman with the tattooed tit howled for more liquor. She was now flanked by Hans on one side and the looming man on the other. Her haughtiness was vanished, and she was stroking the thigh of the looming man as Hans looked on ardently.

"I wish I didn't have my period," she slurred.

Louie took their glasses and went to fill them. "Ain't this somethin'," he said. "Blood runnin' at both ends of the bar."

"What's that?" The voice of the lollipop girl interrupted his mumbling. With a sigh, he turned to see what she was pointing at on the wall behind him.

"It's a license to sell cigarettes," he said.

"Oh. How come you have a cigarette license but no liquor license?"

"It's a long story, and it's not fit to tell to little girls who still believe in Bruce Springsteen and the Easter Bunny."

"I only believe in Liberace," she said coyly. "I believe that he will walk again among us. And the blind will see and the lame will walk. And this big, fat Irish creep next to me will stop staring at my tits."

He brought the three drinks down to the tattooed lady and her friends.

"You like the masturbation?" Hans was asking the looming man.

"Say what?"

"I *love* the masturbation," Hans enthused.

Somebody kicked the jukebox. "You fuck!" somebody else yelled. "That was my record playin'." The famous actor stirred from his slobbering reverie. Standing, he gathered his money except for a ten-dollar bill. He patted Goo-Goo's back, and he staggered out with a wave of his arm. Only then, as he made his way through the crowd, did anyone recognize him.

"To be or not to be, eh?" Louie yelled after him, returning the wave. He knew the actor's tip would be safe on the bar as long as Goo-Goo was there.

The din of the waylayers and the waylaid rose to engulf Louie in waves. Letting his eyes roam as he worked, he could descry, among the lunatics and drunkards and punks, the mingling slaves and lords of every sin of every circle of hell.

A man with the mark of the squealer beneath his eye skulked through the place in silence, seeming in the dense shadowy smoke to vanish and to reappear, now here, now there, like a spectral apparition. The one with the blood on his shirt, death's fair boy, began to bleed again. A long-haired man with a face the color of tallow sat with his eyes fallen shut, maundering torpidly to a woman who was no longer there. The subject was suicide. Near him, two pretty ladies laughingly wondered where they were. A sinister old nightwalker, who knew only too well, grinned and moved nearer to savor their scent.

Through the waves that crashed down around him, there was a siren's song—a seductive call to abandon himself to the billows of oblivion and debauchery through which he steered. He looked to the lollipop girl and he looked to the quart of Dewar's on the shelf; and the song of the siren swelled. But Louie stayed tied to the mast by the thongs of his will.

As six o'clock approached, the pale glow of dawn began slipping through the curtains. The crowd started, at last, to dwindle, and the waves began to lull. Soon each drunken voice, each cough, each lonely laugh became more distinguishable, a stark and solitary note in a forlorn decrescendo of scattering despair.

Goo-Goo, adjusting his cuffs and his collar, the knot of his necktie and the tilt of his fedora, rose and heeded the summons of daylight. The tattooed lady and the looming man and art-loving Hans were gone. So, too, was loathsome Grogan, flustered in his fruitless pursuit of the lollipop girl—who now also, to Louie's chagrin but not to his surprise, was gathering herself to leave.

At half past six, Louie announced last call, and he pulled the cords that dangled from the two fluorescent lamps above the bar. The harsh, sudden light provoked the undead to move. Sniffling, bleeding, giggling, and gasping for air, they stumbled toward the door. Those who stayed for last call shrank from the light, as if hurkling from awareness of their own ugliness. One by one, and in pairs, they finished their drinks and left.

As these stragglers departed, new faces began to arrive and to be served. Most of the stragglers knew that last call meant not that the place was shutting down, but that the place was changing. It happened every morning at about this time. The regulars were used to it, and only a few newcomers were foolish enough to complain. Besides, most did not want to stay beyond this time, for the faces that began to arrive at this time of the day were not the sort of faces to which they were accustomed or with which they were comfortable. Even the little *giovanostri*, the tough-talking, swaggering young hoods who seemed to embody the moviegoers' fanciful notion of the evil in these streets —even they, who frightened the other punks, shied away from these faces, the eyes of which silenced them and stripped them of bravado and sundered their delusions.

They were the faces of men whose own power gnawed within them like cancer, faces that had been recast by the renunciation of all trust and all love and all goodness. Some of them were familiar to Louie. Others were the faces of strangers waiting to do business, or merely to pay their seasonal respects, behind the black curtains nearby. For the most part, these men drank coffee. Some ordered coffee with a shot, and a few just had a shot. The majority of them were well dressed. Louie noticed that about these men; they seemed to take a special pride in being impecca-bly groomed at this hour of the morning, when most peo-ple, headed either to or from bed, looked like shit.

A few of the more familiar faces asked Louie how he had been and how his uncle was. Most of them communed among themselves, in pairs, in a medley of murky dialects —*sciaccatano*, *palermitano*, *napoletano*, snatches here and there of *pugliese* and *genovese*—resorting to *broccolino*, the universal tongue of Brooklyn, when all else failed in their attempts to give voice to their bile. Some just sat in forbidding silence, sipping and smoking and looking at the clock.

Louie drew back the curtains and set the door open with a wooden jamb. He saw, parked up and down the street, the big gleaming Lincolns and Cadillacs and Buicks some of these men had driven here. In several of the cars, drivers sat waiting, reading papers, chewing gum, smoking.

Entering, too, treading softly and obsequiously among the faces of stone, were the drudges and factotums, the scavengers and dregs—the numbers runners and book-makers, the legbreakers and happiness boys—of their world.

In time, the figure of Il Capraio, in his dead father's ugly clothes, appeared outside the open doorway. He stood expressionless for a moment; then he was gone. Four of the racket guys at the bar got up and left. Ten minutes later, they could be seen crossing the street, splitting into two pairs, as the drivers of two identical Lincolns stepped out and swung open the rear doors for them. Then others left the bar; then others after them.

When the racket guys were gone, the hags started coming in for their coffee. Louie heard three different prognostications—all equally horrendous—of what malady Giacomo's hospital tests would reveal.

"They're gonna cut right here," one of the women said, pointing to a blob of uncomely fat that protruded from beneath her ribcage, "and they're gonna find a lump the size of an eggplant." She shuddered theatrically. "I just pray to God it's not malignant."

"No," another said, shaking her head. "It's his heart again. This time, he'll have to have the bypass. At his age, it won't be easy."

Then the third hag, who was the fattest and oldest of the three, and who smelled the most of Shalimar, drew a long impatient breath through her meaty nostrils. She was, Louie knew, the chief medical expert among them. Her knowledge of diseases—firmly rooted in medieval tradition and in the Hippocratic writings of the *New York Post* and the *Enquirer*—was legendary in these parts. There was no blemish of the skin, no passing twinge of pain, no slight increase or decrease of weight that she could not construe as a symptom of some terrifying, deadly illness. She spoke of cancers that could be caused by plucking the hairs of one's nose, of "little baby strokes," and of women whose wombs, due to garlic deficiency, simply rotted away inside them, eventually plopping out one day into the toilet "like a piece of putrid tripe." If anyone confessed the fear of a disease to her, her invariable response was "You can die from that. I'd have it checked out if I were you." There were times when, to corroborate her authority, she brought out a large and olden book called *The Century Home Medical Cyclopaedia*, the page numbers of which also served to guide her at times in her number-playing. In fact, a few years ago, when one of her friends had succumbed to lymphatic cancer, she had hit the Brooklyn number for two hundred and fifty dollars, betting half a buck on 197, the page where the lymphatic-disease entries were to be found.

"You're both wrong," she said. "Giacomo's got worms in his blood. You can see them under his skin."

Her companions' eyes widened.

"They burrow through the veins, and they lay teeny eggs, and the eggs hatch; and, little by little, they take over your entire system. I forget the name for it. I'll look it up tonight."

Huffing and plucking at their inner elastics, the women departed. The two remaining happiness boys, after inquiring whether Louie knew anybody who might be at all interested in buying some plastic guns, pushed forward their coffee cups and ambled out into the day.

Louie swept up and loaded the garbage into a big black plastic sack. He tallied the take—a little over six hundred dollars—and stashed it with the bank under the ice machine. He checked out the toilet for discarded gimmicks, and he poured Clorox into the bowl. When the City sanitation truck pulled up, he brought out the black sack and a six-pack for the garbagemen.

He counted his tip money. There was more than a hundred dollars, not counting the fake twenty that bore a dirty picture where Andrew Jackson should have been. He put the money in his pocket, took one last look around, then drew the curtains and the shade, walked out, and locked up. It was half past nine.

A few blocks away, he bought a *Wall Street Journal*, then stopped off for poached eggs and fried potatoes at a Greek joint that seemed to be turning into an Indian joint. He browsed his way slowly to the paper's second section, where the numbers lay. Moving his eyes with slow restraint to the Chicago Board listings in the Index tables, to the bottom line of the S & P 100, he smiled at what he saw.

Outside, he tossed the paper into a trashcan, then walked at an easy pace to the Allen Street dream-hole. All the way, the morning sun cast a golden light.

Willie was already there. Hearing the door open, he removed his feet from the desk. When he saw that it was Louie entering, he raised them back up.

"Goldstick left this for you last night."

Louie took the envelope from Willie's hand. It held a check for a little more than two grand. He folded it and put it in his pocket.

"So," he said, "how's the movie business?"

"It's nice to have a little cake with my coffee for a change."

"You'd do anything for a buck, wouldn't you?" Louie smirked. "You're a walkin' fuckin' moral catastrophe."

"Look who's talkin'. You and Goldstick there passin' envelopes back and forth like its fuckin' election time in the Ninth Ward."

"I guess it's like you say, Willie. It's nice to have some cake once in a while."

"I'm talkin' half a slice of leftover poundcake. You got a fuckin' bakery goin' for yourself."

"Well, I tell you what, Willie. Why don't you buy me out?"

"Are you serious?"

Louie nodded.

"Why the hell would you ever wanna sell out? You got it like Riley here. You don't do shit but stick out your hand and get it greased."

"It makes me feel dirty, that's why."

"Gimme a fuckin' break."

"I ain't kiddin'. It makes me feel dirty."

Louie was smiling, but he was not fooling. That was the joke: He was telling the truth.

"Shit. You were born dirty, my friend. You been dirty all your life. Besides"—Willie's tone changed—"I thought your deal with Goldstick was, you're only a partner till he pays off that eight-grand note you're holdin'."

"Eight grand, two hundred and eighty, compounded monthly at three percent."

"Whatever."

"Yeah, well, I tell you, Willie. In the last two weeks, Goldstick's probably blown more than that betting on how many times per at-bat Dwight Gooden scratches his balls. He could've paid off that note already—or close to it. But he's a guy who has to gamble away every dollar plus a borrowed dime. If he wins, he parlays until he loses. And he just gets worse and worse. It's his religion. Losing is his penance. He goes through life on his knees in a hair shirt, believin' in the big round-robin in the sky. I don't think he'll ever pay off that note. I don't think he'd pay his god-damn gas and electric if his wife didn't beat him with a broom on the first of every month. He'd be sittin' there with a fuckin' menorah and a racin' sheet, callin' in a hundred across the board on Glue Factory in the ninth at Pimlico. No, I'd be surprised if he paid off that note."

"Well, what do you figure your half—along with the note—is worth?"

"I figure my half, along with the note, is worth at least

thirty grand, cash. It'd be worth more if it weren't for the remote possibility that Goldstick might actually pay off that note within the year."

Louie did not mention the other potential hazards that had occurred to him. There was always the chance of being put out of business by a bust, Louie believed; and there was the possibility—maybe it was a probability—that the success of Dreams, Inc., would attract the eyes of those happy faces that Louie, and Goldstick, knew all too well. If it did, those happy faces would either try to wet their beaks here or run this place under with a bigger operation of their own.

Willie was laughing out loud.

"From you," Louie said, "I'd take five down, then a grand a week for six months."

"Where the hell would I get five grand?"

"I don't know." Louie shrugged. "I can lay this in your lap, but I can't do your thinkin'. I wouldn't suggest that you try to steal the money, because I truly believe, my bosom pal, that, as your institutional itinerary of recent years shows, your career as a thief has gone the way of your two front teeth. Anyway, I just thought I'd give you a shot. If it's not you, it'll be somebody else. Think about it for a while, then we'll see what's what."

"I'm gettin' my teeth replaced, you know," Willie remarked petulantly.

Artie the cameraman arrived with two containers of coffee. He placed one on the desk in front of Willie.

"That's what we ought to get down here, one of those electric coffee makers," Louie mused.

"Let's get a castin' couch first," Willie said. "Let's take care of essentials, then worry about luxuries."

"Where's the dog?" Artie yelped. "You were supposed to pick up the dog."

"Relax," Willie said. "I got it all set. The guy with the

dog is chargin' us by the hour. I tried to talk him into a flat twenty bucks, tellin' him we'd let him watch, but he wouldn't go for it. So I figure why pick up the mutt until my niece gets here? Knowin' her, she'll be late. She's the kind of kid that'd be late for her own fuckin' funeral. When she shows up, then I'll go and get the mutt. We'll save money that way." He turned to Louie with a cockeyed grin. "That's somethin' I'm always lookin' to do, save money for the boss."

"But there's no problem with the dog?" Artie pressed.

"No problem. The guy told me what we gotta do. We gotta cement the Milk Bone down with Krazy Glue near where she spreads her legs."

Willie opened a drawer and, with a flourish, took out a large dog biscuit and a tube of Krazy Glue.

"You'll have to shoot at an angle so you can't see the Milk Bone. This guy said if we stuck it up her snatch like we were gonna do, the mutt might take a bite out of her by mistake. He said Dobermans are like that."

"You're usin' your niece?"

"Yeah. I'm her agent. I get fifteen percent."

Louie beheld him in awe.

"Hey," Willie demurred. "The kid needs the money."

Louie nodded in vague disbelief and repeated those words: "The kid needs the money."

Then in she walked, a cute little girl of about sixteen in a short leatherette skirt.

Willie looked at his niece, then he looked at Louie, who was looking at her legs, and he raised one eyebrow, as if to say "*Et tu.*"

"Well, go get the dog," Artie whined. "It's showtime."

"Yeah," Louie said, tracing an imaginary curlicue in the air toward the door with his finger. "Go get the dog. It's showtime."

The nights and the mornings ran together, and the jukebox blared and the liquor flowed and the money came down like rain.

The grotesque kaleidoscope of shifting, babbling faces grew more repugnant as the weekend wore on. The man with the squealer's scar, the tattooed lady, the drunken mick, the bleeding boy, and all the rest—they struck Louie not as a clientele, but as the cast cards of a forbidden doomsaying deck.

The lollipop girl did not return. But there were others: charmers driven into the night by the mares that bore the names of desperation. Some of them wandered endlessly seeking their fathers' cocks, with a hungry womb or a jagged blade. Some wandered endlessly seeking angels, with a hungry womb or a jagged blade. Some merely wandered. Whatever their mare, whatever their search, they all seemed to pass this way. They batted their lashes and offered what they fancied to be the serpent's fruit—a bruised fallen apple, little more, from folly's tree. The longer these charmers sat and drank, the longer they batted and offered, the uglier they got, until finally, toward dawn, their debasement was their only allure. Then they cried or went their way, alone or with whoever threw a slug of hollow tenderness.

They were seducers, yes, but they were not sirens. Their

presence was only the echo of a recurring note in the siren's song of this place. That song was the true seduction. It cut unceasing through the din and seemed even to send lambent colors trilling through the dark, to turn the wheel of self-destruction into a carousel. That song, which was death made pretty, which was oblivion rendered as lovely as a golden spitcurl peeking from a silken crotch, or as a breeze; that song, beauty from the windpipes of evil, was the Devil calling Louie home.

In the early morning hours of his last shift behind the stick, he went.

"Fuck it," he told himself, holding aloft a quart of Dewar's, beholding it as if it were the head of John the Baptist, then pouring.

He was still pouring five hours later, sitting alone at the end of the bar, when Giacomo shuffled in looking the same as he had looked when Louie had last seen him. Even the ash of the cigarette that dangled from his mouth seemed to be precisely the same length and to droop at precisely the same angle as it had a week before.

"It's alive," Louie intoned, peering into the old man's spectacles.

"It's drunk," the old man intoned in turn, glancing from the Dewar's bottle on the bar to Louie's eyes. He went behind the bar and poured himself a small amount of brandy; then he sat down next to Louie.

"That joint's a fuckin' bughouse," he said after taking a sip. "This guy in the room with me, they wheel him out on the table, wheel him back in eight hours later. He's grinnin' from ear to ear. 'I flunked my autopsy!' he tells me, 'I flunked my autopsy!' I'm lookin' at him, wonderin' what the fuck is goin' on. What he meant was his biopsy was negative." The old man shook his head. "Then they stick me with this fuckin' doctor who looks like two weeks ago he was ridin' around on a bicycle throwin' Chinee take-out menus into hallways. 'Breed deepree,' he says. I tell you, Louie, never again."

Louie snorted a laugh, and he poured from the bottle to the glass, and he drank.

"So," Giacomo said, in a more familiar tone, "how'd we make out?"

"Twenty-six hundred and forty-something. That's minus my deuce."

"Not bad, kid. Not bad at all. Did you do all right with tips?"

"No complaints."

After a while, the old man went to the ice machine. With a terse groan, he bent to where the money was. He rose, groaning again, with a handful of it. He placed it in front of Louie.

"Here," he said, "buy a house in the country."

It was noon when Louie left that place. His body was electric with booze, and his vision was white around the edges beneath the glare of the sun. He could go home or he could continue drinking, he told himself. He looked down at his striding feet as if they were the autonomous arbiters of his direction. He looked up suddenly, in stern affirmation of that noble flame of God-given will that existed within him independently of his feet and shoe leather. Pretending that the half quart of Scotch inside him had not already risen in tyranny to the throne of his being, he savored the delusion of his freedom of choice, then decided on the inevitable. He would go home, then he would continue drinking.

He showered, put on a gray suit and a black silk shirt, stuffed his trouser pockets with money—fifties in a golden money clip in the left, twenties and tens in the right, a lone quarter in the back, as was his custom—and, his heartbeat strong in his ears, was back on the street within an hour. He walked directly to Mona's and he sat down and he nodded once to the unspeaking bartender, and the bartender, nodding back with immediate comprehension, put ice into a glass, filled it most of the way with Dewar's, then topped it off with water.

"Back on the tiles, eh?" he said to Louie, placing the drink in front of him.

Louie drank and beheld the other customers. The faces never changed, he thought. Stay away from a joint for days, for weeks, for years even; come back, and the same characters would likely be sitting in the same seats, drinking the same drinks, saying the same shit. It was amazing, it truly was. They hailed him, and he hailed them in return, despising them—or, maybe, despising that aspect of himself which he saw mirrored in them. They were all glad to see him drink.

The single-action guy entered in his usual huff. To be the single-action guy, Louie felt, was to suffer a fate not unlike slavery. Rushing day after day between designated post times, from bars to clubs to newsstands to the docks to that black-curtained place, around and around again, in rain, in scorching heat, in hail, in snow, all for nothing—a tip here, a tip there—until whatever immense gambling debt had brought his fate upon him was decreed by those behind black curtains to be paid in full. It took years sometimes. By then, the runner as often as not was reduced to a true *schiavo*, a true slave, unable to live any other life. The current guy, Joey, a man of about forty-five, had been at it now for more than two years. So far, he had lost twenty pounds, developed rheumatism, and gone completely gray.

"Two! *Due!* A deuce!" he announced. "The first is a two!"

A few of the customers threw up one hand and cursed, then reached in their pockets for more money. With one eye on the clock, the single-action guy hurriedly wrote down their bets and took their cash. Louie handed him a twenty.

"Twenty on the seven," he said.

The single-action guy scurried out into the breeze, and talk in the bar turned to numbers. One old-timer remarked that a three had not been the lead digit in weeks. Another lamented that he had been about to bet the winning two but at the last moment had changed his mind to four. A young man in a blue Parks Department shirt swore that he would end his single-action betting if the six did not come in next. The fat lady diagnostician from the Street of Silence, who sat at the far end of the bar gulping short beers and violently turning the pages of a *Post*, looked up as each man spoke, shooting invisible poison darts at him with her eyes. When she at last noticed Louie, she waved and smiled warmly, then, looking down at her paper then up again toward him, shot a few furtive darts his way.

Louie did not mix with the others. He sat drinking by himself, luxuriating in the numbing exhilaration of the Scotch. This, the long slow-swelling overture to shit-facèdness, was his favorite stage of drunkenness. The world, which was out there somewhere, stood at bay; and with each swallow he took, the world became lovelier in its obeisance to him. The God of the Old Testament smiled down upon him, telling him he could do no wrong. He was at one now with the siren's song. Like the world itself, Scylla and Charybdis, she who rends and she who sucks to death, grew lovelier to his mind with every swallow. Soon he would raise his glass to them, and would tell them they had pretty hair, and lie upon them. It was—the door flung wide; the single-action guy pointed to Louie, winked, proclaimed "Seven!"—like the second digit, written in the wind.

The single-action guy counted out a hundred and sixty dollars onto the bar in front of Louie. Louie gave him ten, telling him to buy himself a few drinks later on, then he gave him two twenties, saying "Forty on the nine."

At the other end of the bar, the fat lady, whose eyes had followed the counting out of the money with an envy that could not be concealed, broke into a warm smile from which venom dripped. She lifted her beer in congratulations. "I'm happy for you, son," she said in her finest bullshit maternal manner, then gulped down her beer to make ready for the one Louie surely would buy her.

Louie smiled back at her in kind, and through closed teeth he mumbled, "Bleed to death from your cunt, you old witch." Then he bought her one. He bought everyone one. The bartender looked at him as if he were wearing a jester's hood.

For a while, Louie entertained the notion of calling Donna Lou. In the end, he decided to wait until night, when the omniscient, omnipotent booze within him would be in full control, bringing clarity to his evil eye and righteousness to his words and ways. Besides, the Devil told him, anything might happen between now and darkness: That imagined Donna Lou, the perfect Donna Lou, might sashay in with wetted lips and oblation in her eyes.

Louie sat there and drank until a little after five o'clock, when the last digit came in. It was a nine, as he had said it would be. The single-action guy, neither smiling nor frowning, counted out three hundred and twenty dollars onto the bar. Louie gave him twenty, then, handing him two fifties, told him to put it all on the one for the lead the next day.

"God bless you, son!" The fat lady held out her beer and gulped it down.

They all raised their glasses to him, even those he did not know. His response was to lift the palm of his hand to them in a staying sign. Then he finished his drink, left a five on the bar, and strode out into the melancholy light of dusk. He stood still for a few minutes on the sidewalk, acclimating himself to the fresh air, then he turned east.

"Eat!" he commanded himself in a stentorian voice as he took his first step, causing some startled passersby to recoil.

He watched his shoes march with surety to Cent'Anni. He sat down at a table for four. A waiter began to ask him to move to a smaller table, but the owner of the restaurant, who knew Louie, brushed the waiter aside. A more familiar waiter brought bread. Without looking at the menu or waiting to hear the specials of the day, Louie ordered a Dewar's and water, a large bottle of mineral water, a bottle of Brunello di Montalcino 1976, *crostini*, a mixed salad, a small dish of *risotto di frutti di mare*, roast pork with spinach and fried potatoes, and a check.

Forty-five minutes and a hundred dollars later, he left the wine unfinished on the table and stalked back out into the slow-falling sunset, belching magisterially. His shoes took him to Thompson Street.

"I heard you hit the single action," the bartender said before Louie had fully settled onto his seat.

This neighborhood never failed to amaze Louie. It was a neighborhood where, at any given time, at least six people seemed to know what color underwear one was wearing. Once, a few years back, Louie had eaten breakfast before dawn in a greasy spoon nearby where he was the only customer. Later that day, two different men had asked him "How are the eggs in that joint you ate at this morning?" It was as if that Masonic eye that hovered atop the pyramid on the back of the dollar bill hovered over these streets as well. Yet the uncanny all-seeing, all-telling nature of this neighborhood was a boon as well as a curse: Wives here were surely among the most faithful, or the most stealthful, in town.

Louie sat and drank for about two hours. He was now well into his second quart of the day, and, freshly fueled by the meal he had eaten, he grew loquacious. Starting with comments on the upcoming football season, he and the barman proceeded—quite naturally, it seemed—to a discussion of why each succeeding Kennedy was a worse scumbag than the one before. That led—again quite naturally—to a dialogue on the current state of locally available basil. From there, the talk turned to the problem of creeping lesbianism, then to the need for a return to the Latin Mass, and finally to the irrefutable facts that, one, the archbishop and mayor of New York were both stone-cold faggots and, two, the pork chops at Ottomanelli's weren't what they used to be.

By the time they got to the pork chops, Louie was, by his own verdict, drunk. He decided to go home, but after walking barely a block, his shoes halted. Reasoning in a leftward way that lay beyond the realm of logic, he told himself that he would not be drunk again for a long time, so he had better make the best of it. He stuck out his arm, hailed a cab, and went uptown.

It was almost midnight when he left Joe Allen's, and he could not remember the name of the woman who was holding his arm. He was sure that she had told him, and he did not want to risk seeming uncourtly by asking again. Besides, what did it matter? A rose was a rose was a rose. All he knew was that she was a court stenographer from Brooklyn and that she drank Rusty Nails. She was in her late twenties, he figured, and she was pretty.

"Where are we going?" she asked with an expert blend of feigned innocence and vulnerability.

"Like yourself, my dear, the night is young."

She uttered a sound of girlish glee, perhaps feigned, perhaps real.

They walked east on Forty-sixth Street. Louie reveled in the salacious clicking and clacking of her high heels on the pavement. Every few steps, through his ringing ears, he could even hear the lush nylon rustle of her thighs rubbing together as she walked. He wrapped his arm around her waist, laying his hand on her hip, savoring her sway and the sexy glide of skirt over slip over nylon over flesh. And the Lord smiled down, saying "Attaboy, Louie, fuck 'em all."

They made their way to Rockefeller Plaza, and they rode the elevator to the Rainbow Room, a place where Louie, in his right mind, would never go. She, the nameless one, spoke of being hurt in love, and he—heh, heh, heh—consoled her with the shoring wisdom of his soul. When the Rainbow Room closed, a little after one, they took a cab to Clarke's, on Third Avenue. Women, Louie knew, liked going to manly places, especially those manly places where the men plucked between their eyebrows and sucked on little onions and olives. At least Clarke's, of all such places, had good bartenders. It also had what was perhaps Louie's favorite urinal in all of New York—an ancient and marbled walk-in model that might have been designed for the great Zog himself.

By the time they left there, at about two thirty, Louie was speaking in slurred elliptical sentences and the nameless one's eyes seemed to have turned to glass. They went to one more bar, a dive farther south on Third.

"Did you know," the nameless one said, "that the Jews say that Lilith was the name of Satan's wife? They say that she had a serpent's tail and that she had sex with Adam before Eve was created."

"Sounds like my kinda gal."

"When I learned that, I asked my mother why she named me Lily. She said she'd always thought it was a pretty name."

Right. Lily. That was her name. And she was Jewish. Or the Devil's wife. Or a court stenographer. Or one of those things.

She crossed her legs. Again there was that lush and lovely rustle. The lizard in Louie's britches stirred, in a sluggish way. He had been swilling Scotch now for twenty-four hours. He knew that soon the lizard would sleep the sleep of the dead. It was time to move.

"I've got a scumbag with your name on it," he said in the tenderest of manners.

"Mmm," she murmured, and a glimmer of life shone in her glassy eyes.

Then there sat Louie in his shorts on his couch, watching Lily get undressed. He liked what he saw—pink slip, pink underwire bra, no stretch marks—and the lizard liked it, too. He reached out and pulled her slip slowly down. He ran his hands around her hips and grasped her ass, drawing her toward him. He kissed her thighs and worked his fingers to where it was warmest. Delicately— as delicately, that is, as could be managed by a woman who could barely stand—she moved away, lifting her forefinger to suggest a momentary pause. With eyes that were beginning to droop shut, Louie watched her go to her purse, which lay by the door. She stooped and reached into it, then rose and turned with a weird little smile. There was something in her hand.

Shnap! Gleaming metal sprang from pearly black.

"What the—!" Louie's eyes suddenly opened wide, and he clutched the arm of the couch to raise himself in a bolt. But the switchblade was now turned around in her palm. She held the blade and was offering him the handle.

"Where's the bedroom?"

He took the knife from her and led her to the bed by her bra strap. He stood over her and waved the knife.

"What did you want to do with this? Whittle my dick into a Campfire Girl project?"

"No," she whispered in the darkness. "Hold it to my throat."

"What if my hand slips?"

"Don't let it."

"Do you always do this on a first date? I'm surprised you lived to make it through your first box of tampons."

"I trust you."

"You trust me."

"Yes, my love, I trust you."

The way she said it, it sounded like the dirtiest thing Louie had ever heard.

The lizard had shrunk back a bit, as if to say "Let's think about this one a minute, old pal." But then the lizard was in her mouth, and then inside her belly.

"The flat side," she panted. "Press the flat side to my throat. Under my chin. There, yes. Oh, my God, my darling, yes."

She moaned like a chain-rattler, lowed like a milk-cow kicked by a mule. As numb as the Scotch had rendered him, Louie could feel the temperature rising inside her. It was a burning heat. Slowly, the moaning and lowing became a deep whispery incantation that wove through the sounds of her rushing breath.

"Fuck me," she chanted. "Fuck me with that big fat cock of yours. Fuck me."

Her eyes opened and gazed into his, then her whole body shook, then went limp. Instantly, she turned back into a court stenographer from Brooklyn.

Louie moved the knife from her throat and, raising himself but staying inside her, he shut it and locked it; but he kept it in his hand as he came back down upon her.

"I came,'" she said, as if announcing her presence at a charity luncheon.

"I don't give a fuck if you came." He laughed in a gentle way.

She sighed deliciously.

He plunged and pounded, rolled and thrust, torqued and strained, dallied and thrashed. His heart, it seemed, was about to burst; but the lizard would not spit. With a curse, he felt it wither in her molten, many-splendored, stenographic thing. He lumbered from her, and, with what remained of consciousness, he tucked the switchblade under the mattress where he lay.

When he woke up coughing the next afternoon, she was

gone. He put two fingers to his cock, then raised them to his nose to help him remember whether or not he had gotten laid. Then he rose and poured himself a drink. He looked at the telephone. The receiver was lying off its cradle. Had he removed it on purpose or by accident? He could not remember. His suit, silk shirt, underwear, and shoes lay in two heaps on the floor. He went through his pockets for money—there was a lot of it, so he figured whatever-her-name-was had not robbed him—but otherwise left everything on the floor. He did not shower and he did not shave, but he brushed his teeth and splashed his face and balls with Old Spice. Then he dressed: another suit, another silken shirt. He was putting his money into his pockets when he saw the note lying near the ashtray.

Off to serve blind justice. Oh, what a night! Let's do it again! Couldn't find my earrings or knife. Please call if you do.

Lily

There was a telephone number and a rather striking little drawing of a heart with a switchblade through it.

"She wants to do it again," Louie mumbled, then put the note in his back pocket, the pocket where he kept two bits.

There was another note waiting for him at Mona's. It was a less romantic note. It said CALL WILLIE. After giving him this, the bartender reached into his pocket and handed him a wad of money—eight hundred dollars in fifties, twenties, and tens. Louie looked at it, bewildered. Then he remembered. He had bet a hundred on one number or another for today's lead. It must have come in. As he put it in his pocket, the fat lady at the far end of the bar did not even venture the falsest of smiles. All she did was grimly nod his way, as if declaring to the Fates that vengeance would be hers.

After his third Dewar's and water, Louie took a quarter from his change and called Willie at Dreams, Inc.

"I got the five grand," Willie said.

"That was fast."

"Like the man says, he who hesitates is lost."

"I'll meet you down there tomorrow morning. Have the money with you."

"No problem."

Louie nodded silently into the receiver.

"You all right?" Willie laughed.

"Not in the head."

"That's what I figured."

Then the day became a blur and faded into night. There were cab rides and hundred-dollar bets, laughter and commiseration. Though he was hoarse from babbling, the only words of all he spoke that echoed in his mind were "Fuck you...Give him a drink...Give her a drink...Give me a drink...A hundred on the nine." But the nine did not come in, and he did not eat, and he did not call Donna Lou, and the final cab in the final hour of darkness delivered him south.

He moved through shadows, a shadow himself. There was a sudden phosphorescent flash, then laughter. Donna Lou put her arms around him.

"Look." She smiled strangely.

Fat, bloated leeches squirmed on her naked breasts. One by one, she calmly removed them. As she did so, Louie watched her change into his mother, suddenly undead. With joy in his heart, he realized then that his mother really was alive; she had not died.

"Look." She smiled strangely. "They gave me this for you."

In her open hand, there gleamed a large and golden ancient coin. He took it from her, and he felt it become a living thing: a tiny palpitating fetus with tiny trembling limbs. He looked to his mother in wonder, but she was no longer there. In her stead, there was a giant mantis-thing. The fetus in his cupped hand turned to warm liquid. It was not blood, it was something else. It streamed through his fingers and splattered at his feet.

Of course, there was no mantis-thing. He had dreamed it. He had dreamed it all—all but Donna Lou, who now pulled the last of the leeches from her breast. There was a small hole in her flesh where it had gorged, and from that hole, there trickled black bile. The hole widened; the trickle became a flowing. The flowing increased to an outpour, then to a gruesome black fountain that gushed from her body with force. He tried to stanch the torrent with his hand, but it was no use. There was nothing inside her but the spewing blackness.

"So, this is death," she said, in a voice that Louie had never heard.

Then Louie noticed the black bile bubbling from a fissure in his wrist. He turned to run, but, slipping and sliding in the viscid blackness, fell. There were leeches where he fell, and other things. They crawled into his eyes and blinded him, and the only image he retained of all that he had ever seen was a large and golden ancient coin that might have never been. Then the blackness took that, too. He felt death's hand around his ankle, drawing him to it. There was no heaven, there was no hell. There was only this, the blackness; and it had issued from himself.

Slowly, he began to hear sounds in the void. There was the creak of a door. A muffled cough. A distant hissing from old pipes. A melting ice cube clinking to the bottom of a near-empty glass—an avalanche in his ear.

Then he found himself waking—or, rather, being wrenched, by his own manic heartbeat and the noise of his tormented breath. He emerged from the black forest of his inner demons to the amniotic warmth of his stupor.

He sensed eyes upon him. He tried to open his own. It

seemed to take all the strength within him to raise his lids. The first, barest sliver of light was painful.

He cleared his throat, as if to warn whoever's eyes were upon him that he was rising in wrath. Bracing himself, he opened his eyes as fully as he could. Through the haze that veiled his vision, he perceived to his left a mouth. A woman's mouth. He gazed straight at it, his brows raised crookedly, trying to focus. The veil evanesced, and, as it did, those lips painted the color of blood parted ever so slightly, full and wet, in beatific clarity. He was looking at the perfect blowjob mouth. He was alive. And as his face relinquished its funerary mask in the wondrous realization of that fact, the loveliest tip of a tongue peeked from the corner of that mouth and licked delectably at an invisible droplet on its upper lip.

Louie raised his gaze to the eyes above that mouth. They were the most beautifully green and enchanting eyes he had ever seen. They were emeralds and raindrops and purity that begged to be ravaged. He looked then upon the whole of her—at least, that is, upon all he could see without bending over and looking around under the turn of the bar. Her skin was pale, but not in the modish way. It glowed with a certain rosiness. Her auburn hair was thick and long and fell in soft, voluptuous waves. Her nose was noble, and her tits were big—but not so big as to vulgarize the symmetry of her slenderish figure. She was about thirty, maybe a little older.

And, all the while, as he browsed her with what must have looked like a ripper's eye, she calmly beheld him in turn.

He nodded to her gravely, as if deigning to apprise her of his recognition of her charms. He regretted this gross arrogance immediately; but, just as immediately, he ceased his regret, for she not only nodded in return, but smiled and raised her glass to him.

Louie looked to his own glass, whose falling ice cube had

resounded in his ear. Giacomo shuffled toward him to fill it.

"*Love is like a cigarette...*" he lilted, barely audibly, through unmoving lips.

It was ten to nine. The place was empty but for Louie, Giacomo, a lone unsmiling fedora, and her. Had Louie not been in delirium's way, he should have wondered what a woman such as she was doing drinking at this hour in a joint such as this. Instead, however, his only thought, the spirit and sum of his intellect, was: Her legs, her legs, I got to see those legs.

Giacomo patted the bar beside Louie's filled glass.

"That's on this nice young lady here," he said.

Louie lifted the glass to her, then sipped.

"My name is Lou," he said.

"Mine's Shirley."

"What do you do for a living, Shirley, if I may be so bold as to ask?" He spoke impeccably, all but exhausting his mind with the Herculean task of maneuvering the boulders of enunciation into place.

"I'm a reporter for a great metropolitan newspaper," she said. "And what do you do?"

That was a good question, and Louie pondered it.

"I'm a stock-index-futures analyst," he responded at last.

Giacomo looked at him as if he expected to see his nose grow.

"Actually, I just transferred here from Boston," she said, seemingly quite sober and seemingly eager to talk. "I worked for the *Globe* there for ten years. Six months ago, I was offered a better job here, but it took me that long to find an apartment here. I just moved in last week."

"Are you wearing a skirt?"

"Yes," she answered with a quizzical grin. "Why?"

Louie shrugged.

"I like this place," she said.

Louie nodded. He had better start talking, he told himself; otherwise, this broad's drawers and his bedroom floor would never meet.

"There are many interesting places in New York," he said, as if addressing a busload of visiting Rotarians. If the lizard could have bit him, it would have done so then. Immediately, he moved to atone: "Let's—"

"I'm gonna get a fuckin' putty-gun and fill it fulla lye and pump it into that fuckin' lawyer's asshole!" roared the unsmiling fedora suddenly to Giacomo, who tried to calm him with a reticent nod. Then the fedora looked down to the end of the bar. "Excuse me, ma'am. Excuse me, sir. Excuse me, Jocko." Then he was silent again.

"Let's get out of here," Louie resumed.

They caught a cab, and Louie directed the driver to Allen Street.

"I'll only be a minute," he said.

When he entered the basement, Willie and Artie were bent over a frail-looking girl who lay naked on the dingy cement floor. Her ankles and wrists were bound with coarse manila rope; black scarfs gagged and blinded her. Among the knots between her ankles, the two men were adjusting a grappling hook that hung from a gleaming steel chain-hoist affixed to an overhead beam. Stepping back, they heaved like dungeon Inquisitors. There was a ratchety creaking, and, slowly, in wrenching increments, the girl's body was raised up, feet first, into the air. There was an anxiety, a dread, manifest in her that the black scarfs did not conceal.

Willie and Artie nodded to each other; then they lowered her down. She was trembling, and through the scarf that gagged her, she was gasping.

"It's good for the circulation. It'll make your cheeks rosy," Artie said lifelessly, then turned away.

"You look like an advance man for death," Willie said to Louie.

The three of them moved toward the desk.

"You're being bought out by a, a—what's that word, Artie?"

"A consortium."

"Yeah, that's it, a consortium. Me and Artie and our silent partner. Right, Artie?"

Artie nodded with newfound entrepreneurial aplomb.

"What silent partner?" Louie wanted to know.

"Artie's Uncle Sammy. He's—"

"Samuel," Artie corrected.

"Right. His Uncle Samuel. He hit it big out in Queens with the Kabbage Kids Kandy Kompany. That's with all *K*'s," Willie added percipiently. "That's the secret of success, he told us—use a lot of *K*'s."

"Just give me the fuckin' money," Louie groaned, watching the girl twitch gruesomely on the floor.

Back in the cab, he counted the five grand a second time while the lovely reporter from the great metropolitan newspaper keenly watched.

"Well," he sighed, tucking it away, "so much for foreplay."

In his haunted bed, without taking off his shorts, he fucked her twice—once in the cunt and once in the ass. She was menstruating, and when it was all over, his fly was framed in blood.

"My fiancé thinks anal sex is degrading to women," she said, smiling, hooking up her skirt.

"I should hope so," Louie replied. "Why else would anyone do it?"

In Mona's, unwashed, unshaved, and bloodstained, but doused with Old Spice and wearing yet another suit and another fine silk shirt, Louie added Lois Lane's name and number to his back pocket. Kissing her on the cheek, he bade her good-bye and good luck.

"Come on, Romeo," the single-action guy rushed in, "cut the smoochin' and throw me a bone. I gotta live, too."

Louie bet a hundred on the seven. He ordered drinks all around. He lighted a cigarette, took a long swallow of liquor, and watched the clock on the wall erase the passing moments of his one and only life. He asked the bartender what day it was; the bartender told him it was Wednesday.

"Come here, George."

It was the Polack, the one with the sick dog and the lien on his pay.

"Don't look at me that way, Louie. We're straight."

"I just want to talk to you a minute."

The big Polack stood beside him.

"What?"

"Remember, awhile back, I told you that you should kill yourself?"

The Polack sighed and looked away disgustedly.

"How come you didn't do it?"

The Polack shook his head. His eyes were so dead that his hate for Louie and for himself did not even show.

"I'm just curious, that's all."

"You finished?"

"No. Buy me a drink."

"I'm broke."

"You're always broke. Put it on your fuckin' tab."

The Polack did as he was told. He bought a beer for himself, too. In walked the two swarthy little men whom George had seen give ten-dollar bills to Louie on the day Louie had advised him to kill himself.

"Hello, my pygmy friends!"

They beamed and nodded with inane enthusiasm. Louie patted the back of the one in the SEX MACHINE T-shirt, and he called out to buy them drinks. He toasted them with the drink the Polack had bought him. Reaching into his pocket, he gave each of the little men a twenty-dollar bill.

"Free money," he declared. "A Labor Day gift for the noble working man, in whose lowly sweat the great whore, Liberty, bathes her dainty feet."

The little men held the twenty-dollar bills in front of their eyes, mystified.

"Free money," Louie repeated. "Take it. It's an old American custom."

One of the little men jabbered something to the other, and the other's mouth opened. Together, they rejoiced in their wonderment.

"How about a hundred till next week?" the Polack ventured diffidently.

"No," Louie snarled, then smiled. "It would only give you reason to live."

To a thin man at the opposite end of the bar, Louie called out demanding to be paid the money owed him.

"I'm not due for another week," the thin man said, less angry than humiliated.

"I'm callin' it in now!" he bellowed. "I'm closin' out the books."

The thin man looked around, as if seeking intercession.

Louie walked down the length of the bar, and he took the money that lay by the man's drink. The bartender turned away, shaking his head.

Later that day, Louie bought a man's soul for forty dollars and put the contract in his back pocket.

The seven did not come in—not for the first, not for the second, not for the third. The sky outside grew dark, and Louie went to where that darkness took him.

Wednesday became Thursday, and Thursday became Friday. The weekend passed—the working stiffs stampeded through, allaying their impotence with sound and fury and beer—and a new week began. Given seven days, the Lord had made the world. Given seven days, Louie had drunk it away.

He ran out of clean suits and fancy-ass shirts and out of clean shorts and socks as well. For three days, he wore the same blue pants and the same blue shirt, which each day grew fouler with spilled booze and souvlaki grease and stray drops of urine and semen and sweat. One day he tried to shave, and he withdrew from the mirror with bloody cuneiform nicks across his chin and throat. His back pocket bulged and sagged with scraps of paper and unused quarters. Slowly his strength left his body, and weakness and pain seemed to be all that was in him. His mind became a drafty, haunted thing. All around him, people seemed to be whispering against him. An evil was in the air, and dread trickled in his veins. He snarled at strangers—one gave him cocaine in a men's room; another, a blowjob in a ladies' room—and waved away most of those he knew. In the end, few wanted to know him, and he sat in solitary brooding with himself, his one true friend. Then—the sun was going down on Tuesday—he peered through lifeless, bleary eyes across the bar into the mirror, and even he did not want to know himself.

He lurched home, bolted his door, and unplugged his phone. He warmed milk in a pan, stirred some butter into it, drank it down, then stripped and staggered to his bed. There he stayed for more than a day, tossing and moaning, aching and sweating, running scared behind closed eyes through the carnival of the beckoning dead. Finally, the groan to heaven of body and soul subsided, and he slept, drifting darkly, with the august gleam of his uncle's diamond in his eye.

Time to de-drunk the joint," he declared.

He put on his dirty blue pants and his dirty blue shirt and his dirty socks and his shoes. He went through all the pockets of all the clothes that were piled on the floor. He threw the slips of paper and business cards and matchbooks into one heap, the money into another. He put the former into the garbage; counted the latter—there was a little more than five grand—and stashed it. Then he divided the clothes into a laundry heap and a dry-cleaning heap. He walked up two flights of stairs, paused to catch his wheezing breath, and knocked on a door. An old woman opened the door and smiled. Looking into Louie's red, puffy eyes, she understood immediately what he wanted.

"*Si,*" she said, "*un momento.*"

She disappeared, then returned with a bucketful of scrub brushes, rags, and detergents.

"*Madonna mia,*" she mumbled, looking at his laundry heap and the general disarray of the place, "*che pasticcio.*" Then she sniffed the air in an exaggerated way. "*Rabbiosa e cagne,*" she declared: Booze and sluts. She raised her hand to him in mock threat, shaking her head. "*Baccalà, Luigi, baccalà.*"

He left her there, with his keys, and carried the drycleaning heap to a nearby joint whose owner still owed him two payments on a loan. Then he walked to Da Silvano, stopping to buy a *Wall Street Journal* on the way. Though the manager of that restaurant knew him, he took one look at Louie's clothes and sat him in a dim back corner, which was fine as far as Louie was concerned. In the shape he was in, light was no friend of his. He ordered clams and a steak and a big bottle of mineral water; then he went directly to the paper's second section. He found what he was seeking, and he stared at it for a long time, making sure that it was really there.

Grubbing a pen from a waiter, he began to scrawl and to reckon. Suddenly, palpitations of brainless panic shook him, as it occurred to his sickly mind that 315 was a cut number. Then he remembered: There were no black curtains on the windows of the Chicago Board Options Exchange. His heartbeat abated to an irregular slow gallop. He went to the pay phone and made a call.

"Cash me in," he said. Then he ate.

When he returned home, he was greeted by the good piny smells of the old woman's cleaning. His laundry lay in neat array on his freshly made bed. Atop a stack of folded underwear, placed like regal jewelry upon a velvet cushion, were the court stenographer's switchblade knife and earrings, along with assorted coins and a matchbook advertising Park West Dental Associates ("Cavi-Jet Cleaning for Smokers"). The old woman was sitting quietly on his couch, transfixed by "As the World Turns."

"Like you, these people," she smirked. *"Pazzo."*

He gave her a twenty and a ten, and, at the next commercial break, she was gone.

When the wisps of evening came, Donna Louise opened her door to find him standing there, white and coral roses in one hand and a bottle of champagne in the other.

"You."

The months had turned her glare to a stare, her howl to a hiss; but her blue-green eyes had not changed at all, it seemed. They were still as cold and wild as glimmers of a raging sea.

He did not smile his smile of a motherless child, or his smile of demon enchantment. He did not entreat with deceit of any sort. He just stood there, looking into those eyes, holding his flowers and his wine. They felt suddenly absurd in his hands, a fool's common offerings, bought with money instead of blood.

She looked at those things in his hands, and she looked at him, and she shook her head in a slow, damning way.

"What do you want?"

What did he want? He wanted to see light in golden hair. He wanted slavery and its deliverance. He wanted the world. He wanted her. But he did not answer.

There was a little smile on her face. Then, in that smile, he sensed all the venom that a soul could muster.

She heaved, and the door came slamming toward his face. He blocked its slam with his foot, then kicked. The door flung wide and loud, its hinges shivering. Donna Lou recoiled. They faced each other breathing hard. He tossed the champagne and the roses onto the couch, so that his hands no longer felt so much like the hands of a fool. She looked at those hands differently now, but she did not fear them. She inhaled deeply, as if drawing in thunder. Then, after a long moment passed, she spat it out in a gale. He stood there, unmoved, in her storm of execration, knowing that there was more power in his right fist than in all the mouthed words in the world, but knowing, too, that it would be gone from him, forever, that power, spent with a single blow. The thunder gave way to wailing and tears.

"I hate you," she said. There was no rancor in her voice; and that is what chilled him.

But—hate, love—he was not here for words. Their chill was nothing, as fleeting and insubstantial as the words themselves. The human voice, with its thunder and crying and endless weaving of truths and lies spun from the same frail fiber—the human voice was something he had all but had enough of. She saw it in his eyes, as she had always yearned to see it in her own.

Her face was streaked with tears, and he put out his fingers to wipe the salty water from her skin. It took more courage than he thought he had, because he was quite certain she would swipe his hand away. Instead, she touched it lightly with her own, then clutched it, as if she never wished to let it go, as if she never had.

"I've been making some moves," he told her.

"What kind of moves?"

Her voice was a whisper, a breath in his ear.

"Moves," he murmured.

"Come on, Louie." That whisper in his ear lightened, lulled. "It's me, Donna." And it was. She led him to the couch, and she pushed aside the flowers and the wine.

"Stock-index options. I bought a few contracts. I did all right."

She was silent for a moment. Louie turned and saw that she was actually smiling now, not so much bemused, but in a curiously enchanted sort of way.

"Isn't that a pretty complicated thing to just dive right into?"

"They just make it out to be. It's nothin' but the numbers racket with fractions. They go for yield curves and nonsense like that, just like the old ladies with the dreambooks. I figured if I went into it looking at it for what it was—a glorified crapshoot—I'd have an edge over the herd, the ones who believe there's a system to be discovered. It's like any other racket, any other crapshoot, I figured: The smart money ends up taking the scared money the scientific bettors lose."

He explained the details of how it worked, of how, with the Standard & Poor's 100 Index wavering near 300 and with option contracts written at a hundred times the index, or about $30,000, he had bought four call options on margin at a premium of two and a quarter, betting that the index would rise fifteen points in a month. The index, in fact, had risen more than seventeen points in two weeks; and Louie, selling today, would end up, after commissions—the vig—with a profit of more than six grand. This averaged out, he told her, to a little over four hundred dollars a day.

He did not tell her he had decided the index would rise by flipping a coin, or that he had calculated the size of that rise by casting dice.

"Compared to what I've been tryin' to do for a buck, Donna, it's child's play. And it's legal. Don't ask me why, but it is."

For a while, there was only the soft sound of their mingled breath in the falling twilight. Then Donna reached up and hugged him.

"Louie," she said, beaming, "finally, after all these years, you've discovered America."

Midnight married them, as they knew it would; but there had never been a midnight such as this, never, for either of them, a midnight so strange or so blessed. The darkness that held them, Louie knew, was not of this moment, or this hour, or this life. Like the breeze that passed through it, raising the curtains in sighs, it was their temperer. It was what had rendered their flesh kindred, long ago, returned for a span of breaths, to offer salvation or doom. They knew then, both of them, that there was something greater than the storm between them, and that it was theirs to seize and to have, if they took it now, before the breezy darkness was gone.

They gave themselves to that thralldom that bound them. They embraced it and called it love, in the way that

other, simpler slaveries—to air, to food, to the grim con-
fines of the mortal shell itself—were embraced and called
life. Louie reached inside her, and he removed her dia-
phragm and cast it softly to the ground.

J oe Brusher rolled off the hundred-dollar whore and winced: heartburn.

He walked to the toilet, and, with two fingers, he pulled the sagging scumbag from his cock and let it plop into the bowl. He hated them, these slimy things that mired his own prick in his own disgusting seed. He hated them, he always had; but he did not want to get the AIDS. He flushed, then lowered his window to shut out the midnight breeze. A few minutes later, he was dressed, swigging Mylanta II.

He drove the whore back to Manhattan. On their way through the tunnel, she tried to make small talk, but he did not respond.

"Let me off at Leroy Street," she said as the car emerged from the tunnel and turned onto Hudson. "It's payday on the platforms."

"I'll let you off right here," he said, pulling over to make a right. "I paid you, lady, not the other way around."

Il Capraio was sitting alone, clipping his fingernails over an ashtray, when Joe Brusher entered the black-curtained place.

"Got a date?" Joe Brusher said.

Il Capraio did not look up until he was done clipping, and he did not speak until after he emptied the ashtray into a bucket near the wall.

"It's on the bar," he said.

Joe Brusher walked across the creaking floorboards and opened the Florsheim shoebox that was on the bar. Crammed in it were folded wads of twenty-dollar bills, fifty to a wad. With his back to Il Capraio, Joe Brusher smiled faintly as he dislodged one wad, then another, riffling them with his thumb. But then Il Capraio was beside him. "What're you grinnin' at?" he said.

"Nothin'. I was just rememberin' that time, years ago, when the Rat-Catcher stashed that money in the Kotex box. Sonny found it and looked inside. 'I heard of lightin' cigars with the stuff,' he said, 'but this is fuckin' ridiculous. Somebody round here better have a good long talk with their *comare*.'"

"I hated that fuckin' Rat-Catcher."

"I thought you and him were friends."

"Friends?" Il Capraio snorted. "This is my friend."

He placed his right hand on Joe Brusher's shoulders, and, with his left, he patted the shoebox twice.

When he returned home, Joe Brusher put the shoebox in his closet. Then he stripped down to his shorts and socks, and he turned on the TV to Channel 9. It was two in the morning, and there was supposed to be a Paul Muni movie on. Instead, he saw Elvis Presley dancing around on a beach like the faggot that he was. He checked his *TV Guide*.

"Shit," he muttered: wrong night.

He shut off the TV, chased down a little white pill with a swallow of milk, and went to bed. There, as the pill did its work, he drifted placidly, past dying eyes in darkness, toward black and dreamless sleep.

A little more than four hours later, he was awake and making coffee. While it brewed, he showered, shaved, and put on fresh underwear. Then, though he disliked doing so, he did what the doctor had told him to do. He sliced a banana into a small bowl, covered the slices with corn flakes, poured in some milk, and, with distaste, he ate it. After that, he sat and enjoyed his coffee.

He reflected that maybe, after the deal went down and he had moved to that place in the brochure, he would get a maid—a young girl to come in the morning to make his coffee and wash his dishes and scrub his floors and suck his cock. That would be nice. And what could it cost, really, especially down there? Not much at all, he figured.

He had another cup of coffee; then he took the shoebox from his closet and placed it on the unmade bed. From a pocket of an old camel-hair coat that hung in that same closet, he removed five wads of hundred-dollar bills and dropped them also onto the bed. Reaching into the closet again, he brought out a pair of blue pants and put them on. He stood there awhile, making up his mind between a black Banlon pullover and a blue dress shirt. After sniffing the armpits of each, he chose the black.

At a quarter to ten that morning, an hour after he had walked Donna Lou, striding with her head held high and smiling like an angel who had just spread her wings, to the uptown E, Louie got a call from the broker he had telephoned the day before. The contracts, he said, had been settled at 318 ½. He asked Louie what he should do with the money.

Louie, who already had gone through the numbers in today's *Wall Street Journal* and completed the Word Jumble in the *News*, told him to buy platinum and dump it first thing Monday morning.

"I'll let you know then what I want to do."

He went to the couch and he lay down, and he closed his eyes and he tried to scheme. But all he could see in his mind, try as he did to fill it with the gust of his greed, were golden curls and an angel's smile, lighted by an errant ray that Louie had not glimpsed in years and years, a ray of something he could barely half recall: the illimitable wonder of being.

A toss of the coin, a throw of the dice, a rush of hot semen into the womb of the best friend he ever had — these were the coruscations of that errant ray. But neither the falling coin nor the rolling dice could elude gravity's end, that hole in the dirt, the common grave, where every fate converged and fell. Only the seed in the womb could elude. Through it, the silt of souls could flow on forever, long after their shadows were vanished from earth. Maybe that, and that alone, was immortality—a faint lingering, an endlessly fading resonance in the blood of those left behind and those to come. It was a lingering, a resonance, whose source, beneath the dirt, would never feel or know, except perhaps through prescient wisps, here and now, seeing the light of his own eyes, her own eyes, enkindled in the eyes of another. Yet the desire for that merest wisp, that glimmering of enkindled light, had driven him to the womb. Its power was that strong, because it was a desire more of the blood, which was the substance of inherent strength, than of the mind, that gunnysack of mortal weakness and delusion. No miracle ever came from the mind of any man. Miracles came, like all evil too, from his cock, and from the womb—the miracle, or the black magic, whatever it might be, of a soul made in a crucible, imbued by him and leavened by her, brought forth into the cascade of illimitable wonder, where the coin would turn through the air and the dice would roll anew.

The telephone rang, startling him. It was Donna Lou.

"What are you up to?" she asked.

"Just lyin' around," he said, "givin' Socrates a run for his money. What about you?"

"Well, I'm just sitting here, drinking my coffee and waiting for stats, and thinking about how much I love you."

The oldest words, the most worn-out words, the words that had been dragged longer and harder through the muck than any others ever spoken—they were still the best to hear.

"Do you love me?" she asked playfully. Louie could feel her smiling—a cockeyed, giddy little smile, he sensed, the outward bubbling of a deeper beaming.

"Bank on it," he said.

Then, after he laid down the receiver, it hit him.

Yes, he thought, that's it: banks.

J oe Brusher put the shoebox on the table; then from his jacket pockets he took the five wads of hundreds and put them down too.

Giovanni nodded slowly and patted the box.

"That's what he did," Joe Brusher said. "Just like you. Patted it like it was a baby's ass."

"Well, maybe we have that much in common. We both love our children."

The shining black telephone rang like a sacring bell. Giovanni answered it, and Joe Brusher could hear the sounds of a voice, low and vague, on the other end.

"U sacca è piena," Giovanni said into the phone.

Then there was that low, vague voice, and Giovanni nodded once.

"Si," he said. *"Stasera alle sei. Non ti preoccupare di questo. Ernie lo porterà. Si, il negro."*

Joe Brusher followed the old man's words as best he could: *The sack is full. Yes. This evening at six. Don't worry about it. Ernie will bring it. Yes, the black man.*

"Si. Lunedi alle sei e mezzo. Sarò pronto." Yes. *Monday at six thirty. I'll be ready.*

Giovanni returned the receiver to its cradle.

Upstairs, in his apartment, Ernie did the same.

"You're gonna have that nigger deliver our money?" Joe Brusher scowled.

"Yeah. That nigger."

"I don't like it."

"You don't like rye, that doesn't mean it's no good. Me and that man been drinking from the same bottle for forty years. Can you say the same for yourself, about anybody?"

Joe Brusher did not respond, and the old man changed his tone.

"Just relax, Joe. Your work is done, payday's coming. This time next Tuesday, we'll be on the other side."

As Giovanni spoke, Joe Brusher took a plastic vial from his pocket, opened it, shook out a pill, put it in his mouth, and returned the vial to his pocket. He walked into the kitchen, drew a glass of water, and swallowed.

"You ought to lay off that dope," the old man scolded over the sound of the running water.

"It ain't dope," Joe Brusher said. "It's medication. The doctor gave me these."

"Dope is dope. You eat good, a glass of wine now and then, you don't need that shit."

"Look," Joe Brusher said with a harried grin, "the doctor tells me to take these fuckin' things, I may as well do what he says. I ain't got that *albanese* goat blood in my system like you. You say to me 'relax.' Well, these help me relax."

The old man shook his head, and Joe Brusher snorted.

"You know," Joe Brusher said, "it might be a little easier to relax if you let me in on a few things—like how we get two million in cash through Customs wherever the fuck it is that we're goin'."

"Two and a quarter million," Giovanni corrected him. "A million for you, and—"

"A million and a quarter for you," Joe Brusher sighed.

"You like Italian food, right?"

"Yeah, that's what I figured, Italy. But what about the Customs?"

"Joe, at Malpensa Airport in Milan, they don't look at

the incoming luggage unless you have an Italian passport. That's their policy, Joe, plain and simple."

Joe Brusher shrugged and turned his hand ever so slightly. Giovanni, sitting back, peering at him with his eyes strained sideways, could see the deceit all this talk was meant to hide.

"So, like I said, we're set. At six thirty Monday morning, I make my call and give my man the number. Twelve hours later, six thirty Monday night, he gets back to me and tells me where to meet him. I'll call you then. You and me, we'll go together. We'll get our money, and we'll get our asses out of here. The plane leaves at nine fifteen. The tickets are all taken care of, we pick them up out at the airport."

"You ever fly before?"

"No," the old man said. "You?"

"Many a time."

"They say it's safer than riding in a car."

"Yeah. That's what they say."

The old man breathed deeply. More and more lately, his breathing had come to involve effort. He shook his head quietly, in a sort of forlorn calmness, at the realization of this.

"Well, what do you say," he said, "we'll have a shot for good luck. Get the bottle and the glasses. They're in the cupboard over the sink."

The old man poured carefully, squinting and bracing with his left hand the wrist that felt the strain of the bottle's weight. Then they brought their glasses together to make a chinking sound.

"*Alla fortuna,*" Giovanni said.

To that, the both of them drank down their shots in earnest.

Louie and Donna Lou spent the weekend together, and, except for a walk to buy pork chops and steaks, salad greens and wine, they spent it in their underwear.

Louie shared his scheming with her, as he had never done before. He showed her the list he had drawn up of the ten biggest money mills in the world.

"They're all Japanese," she said.

"You got it," he said. "Ten, twelve years ago, the fattest till on earth was the Bank of America, with Citibank right up there behind it."

He blew smoke toward the sheet of paper.

"This country's had it," he said. "Two hundred years, twice around the fountain, and *pft*, down the drain like Babbo. Talk about a quick fuck. From the richest country on earth to the biggest debtor in the world, just like that. No shylock in his right mind would lend this country coffee money on Christmas morning."

Donna Lou was laughing quietly.

"I'm serious," he said, and to a degree he was. "In another few years, the fiftieth anniversary of Pearl Harbor, these Japs are gonna have somethin' to celebrate. By then, they'll have paid us back for those two atom bombs in spades. This country'll still be lookin' up at the sky, worryin' about fuckin' Star Wars; meanwhile, the Federal Reserve Bank'll be shut down, waitin' for a beer-and-wine license so it can reopen as a sushi joint."

"Well, at least, Louie, no one can ever accuse you of floating along with what my cross-eyed college teacher called the Keynesian mainstream of economic thought."

"Keynes, Adam Smith, Milton Friedman—they're all fulla shit. The only one who made any sense was Fields."

"Fields?"

"Abbott and Costello's landlord on TV."

"I always thought Hillary Brooke was why you liked that show."

"That was legs, not monetary theory."

"What was Mike the Cop?"

"I figured he was just sort of a warning to kids, to show them what could happen if they ate too many boiled potatoes and said too many Hail Marys."

She shoved him.

"Let's get back to these banks," she said. "What are these numbers here by the banks' names?"

"Those are P/E's, price-earnings ratios," he told her. "A price-earnings ratio is the price of a stock divided by its earnings per share over the last twelve months. Most people figure that if a stock has a high P/E, it's so hot and so popular that it'll continue to grow. But, as usual, most people are wrong. Buying a stock with a high P/E is like betting a horse that's finished in the money its last three times out. Sooner or later, most likely sooner, the payoff's gonna dwindle. The more popular a horse, the more popular a stock, the less it eventually pays. The trick is to find an overlay, a strong horse, or a strong stock, that isn't being bet down by the grandstand.

"Look at this one, Nomura. It's the second on the list, the second-biggest financial institution on earth. But its P/E is only fifty-four-point-seven, the lowest on the list. Every bank here is a solid investment, but Nomura is the one to buy. Nomura is the overlay."

Donna Lou was looking at him, smiling quizzically and shaking her head.

"Forgive me for asking," she said, "but if you always knew so much about this, why did you wait so long to put it to use? Why did you waste all that time sharking?"

"Well, actually, in a way, sharking and this have a lot in common. The big difference, apart from the thin red line of legality, is that with this you're more likely to actually get paid when you're supposed to. It just took me a long time to figure out that part, I guess."

"I'm glad you finally did. It's a lot nicer listening to you talk about this stuff than having to listen to you curse out the postal system because the bums who owed money weren't getting their disability checks on time."

"Yeah, well, anyway," he sighed. "According to the rules in Tokyo, you have to buy a minimum bundle of ten thousand shares. At about five thousand yen a share, that would come out to something like thirty grand, plus vig. I can't handle that, but what I can handle is an American Depository Receipt for ten grand worth. An A.D.R., they call it. It's sort of a high-class muldoon that you can't get stiffed with.

"So," he concluded, "that is what I am going to do."

He pushed the sheet of paper slowly aside with the fingers of his right hand. Then he slipped those fingers under the elastic waistband of Donna Lou's panties.

"But first," he said, "I am going to run my tongue from your belly button to your yap, with a layover halfway, in the valley of the shadow of your tits."

"Why, Louie," she fluttered playfully, letting herself be drawn down by him onto the carpet. "I dare say that might constitute out-and-out foreplay, punishable by death, no doubt, under some obscure Albanian *lex non scripta.*

"Relax," he said. "What the great Zog doesn't know can cause no harm."

"Here, then"—nimbly, she reached into his shorts—"let me hold your depository marker."

The weekend passed as in a dream. Tranquillity, like a hidden lake, its surface rippled only by breezes of soft laughter or warm conspiring lust, was theirs as it never had been before. Louie fed off Donna's happiness, and she, seeing him thrive on that sweet liquor, glowed all the more in turn. It was not in her Bible, but she knew—though she would never say it—that a soul full of love, a womb full of seed, and a belly full of pork chops were all of heaven she cared to have.

When Monday morning came, Louie made his call. Platinum had opened twenty-two dollars higher this morning than it had closed on Friday. Less the vig, Louie's money had grown by more than three percent while he had been deciding what to do with it. He told the man to get ten grand—his profits, plus part of his margin money—to Nomura Securities on Maiden Lane. A woman named Ellie Dorata would be expecting it. Louie would come by his office later to pick up his remaining money.

"You seem to have done rather well these past few weeks," the man remarked. "If you're thinking about October S & P's, I hope you'll be keeping your account with us. You won't find faster execution anywhere, as I'm sure you've noticed. As a matter of fact, with S & P 500s, we—"

"We'll talk later."

On his way downtown, Louie stopped for coffee on the Street of Silence. He found Giacomo sitting alone at the end of the bar, expressionless, in his vapory cocoon of bluish smoke.

"Lazarus, come forth," the old man cackled through the haze, then was overcome with coughing. It took him some time to gasp and wheeze his way back to composure.

Louie drank his coffee and smoked and peered through the pane. The last rushing waves of summer sunlight were always the most brilliant, the most radiant, flooding forth, then vanishing, then flooding forth again in tidal golden splendor through the somber clouds of fall's first winds. These were the best days, Louie thought, the days of autumn's coming, when the air was sweet with melancholy and the sky became a whirling waltz of breezy dark-blown shadows and glorious bursting dying light. Louie had always felt these things when fall came; and he felt them now, glimpsing the play of sunlight and wind and unseen passing clouds. Then, in the silence, the sound of the old man's breathing seemed to grow as loud as thunder in his ears.

"Something's up," the old man spoke at last, with a curious certainty in his voice.

"What do you mean?" Louie said, turning to look at the profile of that sarcophagal effigy that seemed to have endured a century's weathering attrition in the span of a season.

"I don't know what it is. But it's something." The old man turned his head and gestured in the direction of the black-curtained place. "He's been smilin', Louie. He's been smilin' like he's never smiled before."

"I can't see him smilin'," Louie said. "I can't picture it."

Then the colors of that painting at the bottom of his uncle's stairs overtook the colors of the playing light; and his uncle came to mind.

"Believe me, Louie," the old man said, "you don't want to. You really don't want to."

Joe Brusher had been up since dawn. He had showered, shaved, and dressed. He had reached for the box of corn flakes atop his refrigerator, but his hand had stopped abruptly and he had uttered a sound of disgust. He had taken a pill, gathered his keys, billfold, and change from the ceramic swan on the table by the door, and left. He had driven to Al's Diner and eaten scrambled eggs and sausage, home fries and buttered toast. Then, looking to kill time, he had left his car in the diner lot and walked across the avenue to Lincoln Park.

He ambled toward the benches by the pond where, a long time ago, playing hooky from P.S. 24, he used to sit and spit and waylay other children. The park was nice then. But then they built the projects and told the tootsies they were equal, and, little by little, the park was taken over by the niggers and the spics. It—all of Hudson County, in fact, and across the river, too—was not the place it once had been. Everything changed. Still, he thought, after today, he might never, or at least not for a long, long time, see this place again; and he wanted to remember it.

As he approached the pond, he saw a group of four young black boys gathered at the edge of the dirty water where the pond's pitiful ducks paddled sadly through the debris around their wooden shelter.

There was a miserable squawking. The boys were whacking and thrashing the ducks with branches and a broomstick, and the ducks, in their frenzy, were thwarting each other's escape. The desperate squawking and the boys' high-pitched laughter rose and fell together, weaving through the air.

Joe Brusher stopped and watched. Then he stooped and he gathered up some stones. One by one, he threw them at the boys. The first stone, overthrown, landed in the water, and they did not notice it. The second, underthrown, landed among them, on the paved ground, startling them. As they turned, the third stone hit one of them in the chest. The boy who was hit staggered backward and cried out, and the boy with the broomstick bolted forward a few paces, as if to lead the group in retaliation. Then Joe Brusher pitched the last stone. It hit the forehead of the boy with the broomstick, and he reeled to the ground, drooping dizzily on one knee, as if to genuflect, then keeling over sideways. Joe Brusher picked up more stones and began throwing them at the other boys, who now had turned and started to flee, leaving their buddy on the ground. These stones missed. The boy on the ground raised himself up, wiped blood from his face, and stared at it. In the distance, the other boys, looking his way, moved indecisively. Joe Brusher strode toward the bleeding boy, who, stumbling, tried to get away. But Joe Brusher, breaking into a heavy trot, was upon him. Grabbing the boy by the back of his shirt, he hurled him down and kicked his hip. The boy howled and attempted to rise. Joe Brusher retrieved the dropped broomstick and swung it full with both hands. It cracked with a hollow splintering noise across the base of the boy's skull.

The boy lay face down, moaning and twitching. Joe Brusher rolled him over with two shoves of his foot. Flinching, the boy raised his thin arms and hands over his face and made a begging sound. Joe Brusher saw that blood was still pouring from the pink and purple gash where the stone had struck his forehead. He looked into the boy's eyes. Then he turned and walked away. Nothing was worth remembering, least of all this place.

By the time he returned home, he felt remorse and self-loathing. The sausage, as always, had been a mistake. He should have known better, he told himself. Today of all days, he could not afford trouble in his guts. Cursing himself, he gulped down some Mylanta.

He walked slowly through his apartment, looking around at what he had decided to leave behind, moving as if stalking his own vanished shadow. He owned nothing, really, but clothes, some jewelry, some pots and pans, and the Buick. The jewelry and the clothes he had decided to keep were already packed in the trunk of the Buick, ready for his long drive to Tampa that coming night. From there, after putting his wealth to bed, he would drive south again, to Miami, and from there he would fly to that place in the brochure. There he would need no pots and pans, no camel-hair coat.

Il Capraio called precisely at five that afternoon, as Joe Brusher had told him to do. Joe Brusher was waiting by the telephone, and he lifted the receiver after the first ring. As he did so, he glanced at the box of corn flakes on top of the refrigerator, at its lower left-hand corner, where the words NET WT. 10.5 OZ. (298 GRAMS) were printed in white over the tit of a girl gymnast.

"So, what is it?" Il Capraio said.

"Two ninety-eight," Joe Brusher told him.

Then Joe Brusher took a pill and sat and waited. When six thirty came and the telephone did not ring, he stood and drew breath through his nostrils. He went to piss, but it was only nerves; nothing came out. He brushed his hair, brushed his teeth, washed his hands, and paced. He sat, rose, paced again. At about eighteen minutes to seven, the phone rang.

"Come and get me," Giovanni said. "Our number's out. Our money's wrapped and ready to go. We pick it up at Spring Lake."

Joe Brusher walked to the little table by the door. He gazed blankly for a moment at the ceramic swan, at the chips of faded blue paint that were all that remained of its eyes. Then he opened the drawer, which now was empty except for a small pistol and silencer. He married them, checked the safety, then slipped the gun into his jacket.

"Here I come, old man," he whispered. "Here I come."

With his keys in his hand, he opened the door. From the stairwell to his right, an immense blast of thunderous light blinded him; and as it did, it tore away part of his face, drove burning slivers of his cheekbone into his brain, and blew out his life in smoke and blood through the side of his skull.

Old Giacomo was sitting on a lawn chair in front of his joint, watching the colors of early dusk creep toward the distant big twin towers.

A numbers runner, the little man who drank Cutty Sark and coffee, came through the door of the black-curtained place and waved tiredly to him. Giacomo nodded, even more tiredly, in response.

"What did you hear?" the old man asked him when he was near.

"One-fourteen, Brooklyn. Nine-twelve, New York."

"More cut numbers," the old man mumbled, then turned away, back toward the colors of the dusk.

Il Capraio lived among maternal heirlooms and stolen goods. The maple headboard of the bed in which he slept was the headboard that had shaken in the hour of his conception. The five-hundred-pound Mosler safe beside it, which served as both a bank and a night table, had been hauled out of a Grand Street warehouse and delivered to him by several men whom the trotters had been treating poorly. An old Italian Bible, still containing the pressed flower of his mother's first Communion, lay in a drawer with swag Mass cards and a gross of gold-plated Cartier watches. Indeed, wherever in his rooms his eyes came to rest, he was reminded of his mother or of larceny's wages, or both, as was sometimes the case when he watched the big Zenith TV, one of a truckload, that sat atop the lowboy in which his mother had kept her threads and needles and sewing scraps.

But tonight, at a few minutes before eight, as he turned on the television to WPIX, his mother was far from his mind. He sat and he waited. Then there she was.

"—ten balls numbered zero through nine. The numbers will be selected automatically from left to right, just as they appear on your ticket. Assisting in tonight's drawing is Karen Green. The drawing is conducted and supervised by the New York State Lottery, under the observation of an independent auditor from Deloitte Haskins and Sells."

"Come on, already, speed it up, you bitch."

"And now for tonight's winning numbers."

One of the white bobbing balls popped up into the neck of the plastic gizmo.

"First ball up!"

He leaned forward, straining to see as the grinning girl turned the ball with her fingertips.

"It's two."

His heart hastened wildly.

"The next number—"

Blood pounded in his temples and neck, and in his wrists.

"It's six. And the last number is three, making the daily number two-six-three."

He sat motionless for a moment. Then he stood and went to

the telephone. He began to dial area code 201, but he stopped and instead dialed a local number.

"Get down here," he told the little devilish man who answered. "Get down here right away. I need you."

The little devilish man arrived at Fairmount Avenue in Jersey City just in time to see Joe Brusher's body being brought down the stairs amid a crowd of cops and onlookers.

"I was makin' supper when I heard it," one fat woman told another, raising her right hand to her hair and flapping her left excitedly in the pocket of her smock. "I thought the boiler blew up, I almost died."

The second woman shook her head piteously and made loud commiserating sounds with her tongue on the roof of her mouth.

"He always kept to himself," somebody said.

"Still water runs deep," said the woman in the smock. Then she turned to the little devilish man. "Well," she sighed to him, "let me go wash dishes."

The little devilish man got back in his car, and he drove west to Newark, as he had been told to do.

Louie and Donna were still in bed. Adrift between sleep's undertow and morning's waking current, they were aware of the warmth of each other's flesh, and of the cool pastel light through the window, but of nothing else on earth.

The telephone rang five times before opening their eyes with its sound. They thought it was the alarm clock, and Donna, moaning in response, got up to shut it off. But by then, the ringing stopped. She looked at the clock.

"Who would call you so early?" she asked, slightly annoyed but at the same time relieved to see that she had another thirty minutes to drowse.

"Nobody," Louie said. "I don't give this number to people who drink."

She giggled. It was a groggy, private sort of giggle.

"What's funny?"

"Nothing. You don't give this number to people who drink." She giggled some more. "That's like the pope closing St. Peter's to people who pray."

"Booze and telephones don't mix. I don't call people when I drink."

"Louie, you don't even send a postcard."

She rolled closer to him and started tickling him. It was then that the telephone rang again.

"You get it. I got a hard-on," he said, warding off her frisky fingers.

"'Woe unto them,' I will say"—she gave him one last impish poke—"'that rise up early in the morning that they may follow strong drink.'" She hopped out of bed, threw on Louie's robe, and went to the telephone.

When she returned to the bedroom a moment later, she was no longer smiling.

"It sounds serious, Louie," was all she said.

He looked at her, pulled on his shorts, walked to the other room, and raised the receiver to his ear.

A voice he had never heard before summoned him to Newark to identify the body of his uncle. He nodded fatally, then hung up the phone. Then he sat on the bed near where Donna Lou lay, and he told her what she already knew. She put her arms around him and pressed her lips to the strength in his back.

Louie was going to take a cab to Newark, but then he shook his head grimly at his own blind folly. What was five minutes, one way or the other, to a corpse? He would take the train, and, furthermore, he would not pay to ride. His uncle would have liked that.

He descended the stairs of the Christopher Street PATH station and picked up the emergency phone by the turnstile. He could see the transit cop on the platform curiously eying him.

"Conrail Courtesy," Louie said into the phone.

"Where do you work?" the voice on the other end asked.

"South Kearny piggyback station."

The turnstile clicked, and Louie strolled through it just as the train was arriving.

At the morgue, he was asked to have a seat. He let his eyes wander, remembering what his uncle had told him about this place, about how, years ago, on Sunday mornings, men would shop in the back alley, going through the boxes of shoes and eyeglasses that had been taken from kinless stiffs. As Louie sat there, two bodies were wheeled by within a few minutes of each other.

"You see the way Gooden pitched last night?" one of the black corpse-wheelers asked his partner.

"They shoulda took his ass out in the fourth," his partner responded, turning to look at the legs of a woman who passed by crying into a handkerchief.

"Shit, man, you ain't tellin' me that motherfucker ain't back on that goddamn shit. He look worse'n half these motherfuckers I haul in this goddamn joint."

"And they dead," his partner chuckled.

A blue and ashen hand dropped from beneath the sheet as the cart veered toward the elevator.

"Shit, Claude, look at this shit. You ain't strapped this motherfucker down worth a shit. Look like one them damn Creature Features or some shit."

"Just git in the damn elevator."

A man dressed in white, black and barely older than Louie, stepped from the elevator to the front desk. He then walked over to Louie, introduced himself as the assistant examiner, and sat down beside him. "Your uncle was killed by a shotgun fired at contact range," the assistant examiner said. "The shot was fired into his mouth, and the gun was found on top of him. He either killed himself or was killed in a manner made to look like suicide. In any event, there was no sign of a struggle. He was dead somewhere between twenty-four and thirty-six hours when his neighbor discovered the body. Rigor mortis had passed but decomposition had not yet begun."

Louie felt his stomach sicken. It was not so much what the man said. It was the smell of this place.

"When a shotgun is discharged in such a manner, the shot doesn't scatter. It enters as a solid mass, along with the wadding, through a single wide hole. The gases and fire from the muzzle cause massive disfiguration. It's better that you know this before we go downstairs."

They went below, where it was cooler but where the

smell was more acrid. The body was wheeled into view in its sheet of white, then slowly exposed.

Louie looked down at the one shut and swollen eye, at the torn flesh and bared tissue. He nodded, and then he signed what papers were brought to him. He told the waiting investigators that, yes, his uncle was an old and sick man who had seemed sometimes to dwell on death.

Then he walked out into the September sunshine, and he grinned like a fool.

To the disappointment of the undertaker, who vainly protested that Giovanni's burial-insurance policy would cover all costs, the closed-casket wake, according to Louie's wish, lasted only one day. Flowers came from Ernie and—Louie was both surprised and pleased to see—from Giacomo, and from a handful of others whose names Louie knew only barely or not at all. Il Capraio, who used the same florist that Louie and Giacomo used, sent what Louie recognized as the cheapest of available choices—#D1, the Economy Sympathy Garland—along with one of the swag Mass cards from his drawer.

At the cemetery in North Arlington, on that first day of fall, Louie and Donna, Ernie and his wife, and a few old men Louie did not know stood by as the bronze coffin was laid into the ground and a tall, wan priest spoke by dismal rote of resurrection and the light. They tossed their single roses into the grave, then turned and walked away. Ernie's wife, weeping, lingered a moment in prayer.

"Where'd you dig up that priest?" Ernie asked in a hushed voice as they ambled toward the limousine chauffeured by the undertaker's middle-aged rat-faced son. "He looked like he couldn't make up his mind between a pecker up the ass and a stake through the heart."

"I took what I got," Louie told him. "It wasn't like they

were all trippin' over each other's skirts to get here when they heard his name."

"At least it's over and done with now. The way I see it, that poor bastard in that hole made out pretty good—a two-grand box in a high-rent worm farm. Sure beats potter's field."

They looked back at the grave. Ernie's wife and Donna Lou were coming toward them. The older woman, still crying, held on to Donna's arm as they walked.

"Yeah," Louie said, "I guess so. Whoever the hell he was."

As the limousine wound slowly through the cemetery, they passed another burial in progress. Among the impressive floral displays heaped by the grave, dwarfed conspicuously by the rest, Louie recognized another Economy Sympathy Garland, already blanched and wilted, lying ugly in the morning light.

The car turned onto Route 17. In time, the Manhattan skyline came into sight, dominated by those two immense and dreary cardboard-gray towers. Then downtown Newark obscured it. Ernie's wife, speaking softly, broke the silence they rode in. "Things like this make you think," she said.

Louie nodded distantly and closed his eyes to the sun.

The next morning, while Louie was on his way to have coffee and thank Giacomo for the flowers, he saw Il Capraio in the shadows of the doorway of his black-curtained place; and Il Capraio saw him.

Their eyes met for a moment—for less than a moment, for less time than it took to draw a breath, or to die. But neither man spoke, or made a sign.

Il Capraio watched after Louie, and his eyes narrowed to malign slits. Then he shook his head and looked away.

"No," he muttered to himself. "Impossible."

Louie went directly by cab from Fiumicino Airport to the central station in Rome, and from there, by rail, to Foggia. It was a long and roundabout train ride, begun in daylight and ended in starry dark. He checked into the nearest hotel, the Cicolella, on Viale XXIV Maggio. After a light supper of sausage and beans, he strolled to scrutinize the bus schedule that was posted across the road from the station. There was one bus that traveled the one winding road linking the villages in the hills above Foggia. It left at ten in the morning and returned at eight at night. He walked awhile more, stopped for coffee and a smoke, then went back to the hotel. He slept until dawn, when cawings and pealing bells waked him.

The sky was a wonder, a pink and gray and violet rippling glimpsed in waking through sheer white wind-blown curtains. Through the dewy haze, the hills could be seen, rising among clouds that still bore the colors of night. He stood and watched the orange sun turn it all to day.

The old bus trundled along easily at first, but the higher it climbed into the hills, the more it creaked and rattled and groaned and trembled. Each little town, higher in the hills than the last, seemed to be older and more forgotten by time than the one just passed. At one sharp, precipitous bend, the bus had to stop, reverse inch by inch till its back end jutted out over the steep cliff at the narrow road's edge, then heave forward again to complete the turn. The handful of other passengers applauded mildly. Apparently, it was a routine feature of their journey. All he could see of the village of Castelnuovo were crumbling remains of a medieval fortress hewn into a craggy palisade. Castelnuovo meant New Castle. Beholding it, Louie wondered what Casalvecchio—Old Castle—would be like. Finally, high in the clouds, there it was, the Casalvecchio skyline: a stone crucifix atop a church.

The bus stopped to leave him on a dusty cobblestone road in the shadow of that cross, which was the center of town. Louie walked till he came to the road's end. There was an old monument there, a memorial to the dead of this place. CASALVECCHIO AI SUOI CADUTI, it said: *Casalvecchio to Its Fallen.* Beyond it, there was a cliff overlooking waves of farmland and woods. Louie turned around and went back the other way.

He came to a little bar and looked in. He saw a blue-shirted *questurino* and a fat old man with golden teeth sitting with coffee and a bottle of *amaro* between them. They were talking loudly of the upcoming Giuoco del Lotto drawing.

"Un miliardo lire"—a billion lire—the blue-shirt gushed.

"Un miliardo quattrocento milioni cinquecento mila duecento venti," the fat man sternly corrected him: a billion, four hundred million, five hundred thousand, two hundred and twenty.

Louie walked on, through hens and old women in black. He had never seen posters for funerals before. The sun-baked walls of this place were plastered with them. Then, amid the chickens and the bent-over women in black and the funeral posters and the dust, there was a magical sound: the click and clack of high heels in aimless seductive cadence. His head turned in the direction of that sound, and he saw the most beautiful woman he had ever seen. But, in that turning moment, one of the old shrouded women, watching the movement of his eyes, snarled at him—literally, viciously snarled, in the manner of a lioness protecting its cub. Louie continued on his way.

Beyond the shadow of the cross, there were trees. Within those trees, there was a lovely little garden, and in that garden, beneath the sunlight that flickered through the shady canopy of those trees, there were old benches of stone. And on one of those benches, his uncle was sitting with his eyes serenely shut. Louie walked up and sat down beside him.

"So," he said, "who do you like in the Series?"

The old man jolted slightly, his eyes still closed. Then he smiled widely; smiled like a fool.

"My buddy," he said, and opened his eyes. "I knew you'd come. All along, I knew it."

Louie put his hand on the old man's shoulder, and he shook him gently, grinning.

"I know, I know." The old man waved one hand.

Louie, still grinning, slowly nodded.

"How was my funeral?"

Louie told him about the Economy Sympathy Garland, and the old man's belly and shoulders moved with dry, quiet laughter.

"Did you tell your girl? Did you tell her it wasn't me in the box?"

"No," Louie said, and then he was silent for a moment. "Don't take this the wrong way, but I think she's better off thinking you're dead."

"That's right," the old man said firmly. "A man and a woman making a life don't need blood kin around. Family's just sand in the scumbag when it comes to that, don't let anybody tell you different."

A man some years older than Giovanni ambled by with a cane in one hand and a yellow pear in the other. He raised the pear and greeted Giovanni by name.

"Buon giorno, cavaliere," Giovanni saluted him in return.

"That guy was born right next door to where I was born. He still lives there. 'Where you been all these years?' he asked me. *'L'America,'* I told him. 'What did I miss?' he asked me. 'Nothing,' I told him. *'Niente.* You didn't miss a thing.'"

A blackbird glided down through the leaves overhead, chasing a songbird through the air, then round and round.

"I imagine Ernie explained everything to you," the old man said.

"Pretty much. But he didn't explain why. Maybe you can tell me that."

"It was something to do."

Louie looked at him sideways, and he shook his head and he quietly laughed in his face.

"I wanted to balance the books, Lou. That's what it was. I wanted to make that bastard trust for once in his life and choke on that trust. I could've taken his money *and* his life. But if I'd done that, they would've come for you. Besides, it's better this way. I'd rather have his money than his life. It's worth more. He'll take credit for killing me and Brusher. That's his way. Meanwhile, till his dying day, his ass'll hurt from the fucking he took. And when that dying day comes, God willing, I may still be around to dip into the interest on his money and send one of those—what is it?—Economy Sympathy Garlands. If not, you can do it for me. Set aside a few bucks for that from the insurance money. You and Ernie, you're my beneficiaries. You deserve it, and it'll keep your mouths shut."

"How did you suck in that Brusher?"

"I just told him I had an idea, that's all. I told him about those three zeros, and what happened to me after. I told him the lesson I'd learned from it, that men believe more in a lie, a dream, than in what's real. Then I lied to him. I told him I'd had a new idea. I told him the idea and he believed it. He forgot the lesson and believed the lie. That's the way he was. Maybe that's the way we all are.

"Anyway, nobody got hurt but him. And taking a life like his is like sparing ten. That stiff they snatched from the morgue didn't feel a thing, that's for sure. And he had no use for that face where he was going.

"That's it. I wanted to balance the books and I did. I wanted to sleep in peace. Now I can. Every man's got his lullaby. This was mine.

"And this is a good place for sleeping, Lou. It's a good place to eat and drink and walk and sit and sleep. And there's something about ending up where you drew your first breath, something in the air that makes it sweet for you."

Their talk drifted on, but the lulls grew longer. Neither of them wanted this day to end, but they knew that, like all the rest, it must; and so they resolved to end it with laughter and rob the dusk of its melancholy stole.

Then they sat together, alone in that garden, one last hour, each of them knowing he would never see the other again, and savoring the breeze, the both of them, each in his own way.